REMEMBERING TO FORGET

by Renee´ Richards

RoseDog Books

PITTSBURGH, PENNSYLVANIA 15222

ISBN # 0-8059-9266-9
Printed in the United States of America

First Printing

For information or to order additional books, please write:
RoseDog Books
701 Smithfield St.
Pittsburgh, PA 15222
U.S.A.
1-800-834-1803
Or visit our web site and on-line bookstore at www.rosedogbookstore.com

Remembering to Forget

PREFACE

Regina could remember as far back as the age of eighteen months, though her nightmare of a life actually began before she was born. You see, her mother's life had been in an uproar since age ten but, people of her mother's generation practiced silence about family affairs no matter how much pain those secrets caused.

They were told, "What goes on in this house, stays in this house." No matter how vulgar, obscene, strange or bizarre the happenings, the rule still applied. However, the only way to fully understand her life was to look back before Regina existed, past her mother; back to her grandmother and grandfather Neilson.

CHAPTER 1

Carla Neilson, was born October 14, 1921 in a small town in South Carolina called Florence. She was reared in an old house on McQueen Street, right on poverty's doorstep. She had three sisters and one brother: Pauline, Pansy, Annabelle and Lofton. They would all agree their mother, Ester, was an easy going and well thought of person by everyone. She was half Native-American and had long, wavy, black hair. She was simply beautiful. But, stories suggested that Ester had not always displayed such a gentle nature. In fact, she once beat a neighbor bloody for threatening to spank her daughter, Pauline, who threw a stone and hit the neighbor's son in the head in retaliation. Apparently, the neighbor's son had first thrown a huge rock at Lofton who was sitting on the porch playing. The rock hit the three year old's largest toe on his right foot and caused it to bleed profusely. Carla's mother then took it upon herself to take revenge and she went storming over to her neighbor's house. She became enraged once the woman acted as though it was all no big deal. "That's how children play," she sarcastically responded.

It was customary to wash clothes outside in iron pots under an open flame in the 1920's. And as the children watched, Ester took a stick that she had been using to push the clothes down into the wash pot and struck the neighbor repeatedly with it. Nothing could restrain the rage that was unleashed; not even the sound of the Neilson children as they screamed for her to stop. She was not satisfied until she had beaten the woman unconscious and her bloody body was drug back inside by relatives who occupied the house with her. There were no more confrontations between the two family's because soon after the incident, the strangers moved away.

Carla's father, John Neilson, was extremely tall and possessed the darkest black skin and coldest set of red eyes of any man that had ever lived. They always appeared bloodshot no matter whether he had just awaken or if he was exhausted from a long day of work. People in the town feared him simply because he never smiled. He never said very much, not even to his family members and he never socialize with other people at all. The only evidence of communication with his wife was the three children who were conceived during those intimate times. If he merely presented himself in a room, his overwhelming appearance would make people extremely nervous and their need to leave was immediate. He could definitely clear a room.

But, stories told by Carla gave people reason to be terrified of him beyond his appearance. She witnessed her father take a man by the collar with one hand as he pounded his face with the other and the stranger's feet dangled beneath him. The violence took place simply because the gentleman had found interest in one of John's daughters. After that incident, young men would tremble as they reached the front porch to see one of the Neilson girls, even though the daughters were then of respectable dating age. Prospects knew to first ask for Mr. Neilson and then to ask his permission to speak with whomever they desired to visit. Even then there was no guarantee their request would be approved and more often than not it was denied.

That was what they experienced as a normal childhood and their parents were the only example that the Neilson children could consider ideal. Was Ester and John really to blame for their perception of proper behavior as important role models for their children? Or was the behavior that they exhibited, the only one that they themselves had witnessed? Who can say? There were tales of Carla's grandmother, Mossy, who had the reputation of being as mean as a rattle snake and was known for spitting tobacco juice in the eyes of everyone she disliked. Just about everyone was in that category. But, heredity sure proved to be true in the next generation with John and Ester Neilson.

Carla got along well with her siblings. But there seemed to be a lot of envy for her from her sister Pauline who inherited the hatred and meanness from her father. Carla, Pansy, Annabelle and Lofton were the calmer of the five. Carla shared almost identical features to her mother and possessed the long, wavy hair and pecan tan, smooth skin as well. She carried on her 5'8" frame a shapely body which was analyzed and described then as a "Coca-Cola" bottle by adoring young men. She was extremely intelligent and graduated valedictorian of the Wilson High School class of 1938. She had no desire to further her education, though. All her expectations and greatest hopes for life were to be found in her husband and the family that they would share together.

She was in love with a young man who was several years older than herself, Geoffrey Richards. He was of medium build and height, fairly handsome, dark complexioned with course hair and strong features. To look at him made Carla's heart sing. Everything about the man appealed to her. They married soon after her graduation and she looked forward to a "happily ever after" life of her own. But, things did not go as planned and she found herself disappointed and disillusioned. Children would seem to be her only hope of total fulfillment and yet she still had no realistic idea of what an awesome responsibility and sacrifice it would be to raise a child. After she gave birth on the day before her 18th birthday, the thought of being a mother gave her more pleasure than holding the 1 lb., premature baby, William, who had just been delivered by a mid-wife at her home.

Carla struggled to take care of the tiny infant whom everyone insisted was going to die. Also, the mid-wife was adamant about his death which frightened the first-time mother even more than the little fragile body of her son. He was small enough to hold in one hand but, his will to live and her cautious handling of him paid off in the end. She wrapped him well and kept him constantly under her armpit for warmth because incubators had not yet been introduced. William was the spitting image of his father and as the days rolled by, not even motherly joy could overpower her unhappiness; only her husband, Geoffrey could ease her aching heart. Unfortunately, he did not have time nor interest in his wife, not to mention, of a new father. His mind and time was occupied by women and having a good time. He worked and provided the necessities of the home with consistency and amazingly his responsible handling of the household made Carla continue to love him more deeply with each passing day. Soon, there were two more children born within the next three years, Malvin and Geofreda.

The good times had to come to an abrupt end when Geoffrey decided that he wanted to move north to make more money and to start a new life. Carla really despised the thought of leaving the only support she knew in her mother and siblings. With her mother's encouragement though, she was forced to reconsider. Geoffrey left for Philadelphia first to find work and soon sent for his wife and children. He lived with his brother who persuaded him that good jobs could not only be found, but were plentiful. In hopes that life with Geoffrey would be as she had originally dreamed, Carla packed all of their belongings and headed north by way of Amtrak. As she clung to the hope that the "City of Brotherly Love" was going to be the miracle cure for their ailing marriage, she struggled with three small children as they grew restless nearing the end of the trip. She really had no knowledge of what to expect of a large metropolitan city because she had never been outside of Florence and almost immediately became homesick.

"Oh Lord," she thought to herself as they stepped off the curb in the train station that reeked of urine. It was Tuesday, garbage day, which explained the other fowl stench in the air.

"I have never lived in such a mess in all my born days. I should never have followed Geoffrey here."

She could not be judged by her reaction because Philly's garbage days were neither a pretty sight nor smell by any means. Geoffrey's brother had arrived at the station to pick them up while her husband remained at work. Carla knew that they would only stay with Larry until they could afford a place of their own. He was wearing an old brown derby, a red flannel shirt, a dark blue pair of work pants and heavy duty work boots.

"Nope," she said aloud. "You haven't changed a bit!"

They were relatively quiet on the long ride into the heart of Philadelphia mainly because Carla and the children were exhausted from the trip. The reason for Larry's silence was that he knew Geoffrey had not behaved as a married man with children and did not want the task of careful conversation to protect his brother's lifestyle. Oh yes, you've guessed it, women and partying. But, it was too late for regrets now because the last of the family's money was used for the train tickets and Carla would just have to make the best of a bad situation. It was only a month before Geoffrey was able to place his family in their own home and by that time everyone's patience had been put to the test.

He was an excellent provider and worked on the rail yard making a good living for those days. But, sadly enough, nowhere in that city would ever be home for his wife and once again she had that feeling of complete emptiness and abandonment. When she overheard rumors from the streets about Geoffrey's infidelity, she was sure that she was going to lose her mind and found it extremely difficult to cope with the situation. She decided that she had to confront him so that he would at least know that she was not a fool. But, was she? Even with knowing the truth about him, she loved him even more. She actually loved the ground that he walked on.

"Geoffrey, how could you bring me so far from home and mistreat me this way! I can't understand why you have to have other women and stay out all night long. It really makes no sense to me at all," she yelled.

"What do you know about anything? People talked about Jesus Christ. What makes you think what they say about me is true? Huh? Just you tell me that!" he exclaimed.

"I heard you telling that woman this afternoon that you would be meeting her at the usual place and that you couldn't wait to get to her," she replied through her tears.

"You were listening to my conversation, Bitch? I'll teach you not to listen in on me," he said through clenched teeth as he raised his right hand and slapped her face.

It was not an isolated slap because fist fights were common with those two. Carla decided after the last beating that she was going to fight back and they were always brutal enough to draw blood, normally lasting at least an hour. The children listened to lamps crash, screams, scuffles, and the sound of the blows. All they could do at their age was to listen, cry and pray that the fights would stop and usually they did but with bruises left as evidence of the occurrence. Carla was still a beautiful woman and very shapely considering she had three small children. But not even the long, wavy, black hair could hide the black and blue marks on her face as she looked at herself in the mirror. The sadness seemed even worse. Just from the looks of her, you would have thought that her unfaithfulness had been exposed when instead, she was the innocent one punished in spite of the fact.

"There has to be better days coming for me," she thought as she stared at the image in front of her which was barely recognizable as herself.

In spite of so many women, Geoffrey found time to keep Carla pacified sexually and quickly there were three more children for her to bury herself in. First came her daughter, Carlyle, then her son, Ransell. And last was her daughter Angel. They all were born within a four year time span and had no idea what life was to be like for them as they grew older and watched their parents' relationship. Maybe for them things would be different and either Geoffrey would devote himself to his family or Carla would finally adjust to her husband's infidelity. But, how do you adjust to such a thing? That was a question that Carla did not know the answer to and depression was inevitable.

Even though Carla was an exceptionally clean woman and actually enjoyed keeping a tidy home, the house was in shambles almost on a daily basis. Even her personal appearance started to be of little interest to her. Life no longer had much meaning because she lacked the attention from her spouse that she desperately needed and wanted. After all, he was her whole world. She was in a strange place with no family or friends. So, after six months of wallowing in self pity, Carla decided that she had to make her own life worth living and her sole happiness should not be based on one person. She began to wear a little make-up and treated herself to afternoon movies just to get out for some fresh air in hopes of cheering herself. Actually, the movies served as an escape from the life that had become so miserable for her. Well, it worked as far as she was concerned but Geoffrey assumed that she was practicing his bad habits and those outings caused just as many problems with their marriage as his womanizing. He accused her practically every time she left the house. She relied on public transportation for her get away and had stumbled upon a new found freedom. The more Geoffrey insisted that she stay home, the more she was determined to go.

Geofreda, the oldest daughter, found herself playing mother to the three smallest children. Meanwhile, Carla spent more and more time trying to find herself as she openly experienced life. But the young teen had no problem with filling her mother's shoes at first because she had seen her mother go from not eating and walking around almost dead to looking healthy and happy. What she did not know was that she had to continue to sacrifice her childhood for her mother's rejuvenation. She also sacrificed a mother-daughter relationship which was extremely weak for that stage in Geofreda's life. The depression that had so plagued Carla for years transferred from mother to daughter.

Carla decided that she hated the arguments, the fights and the accusations and over the years, Geoffrey had crossed that thin line between love and hate. She no longer loved him and as a matter of fact, she felt that if someone came to her with news of his death, she would have gladly stood over him and spit in his face. Carla was very uncomfortable with those feelings of hatred and realized that it was time that they parted. There would be nothing to stop her from the attempt to take his life during one of their next battles. Those feelings toward the man responsible for the majority of her grief let her know there was nothing left of that crazy marriage which had been the case for over ten or more years.

Because she had nothing but her school record for a reference and no experience in the work force, she knew that her departure from her husband would mean that it was mandatory to leave her six children behind.

CHAPTER 2

Carla's sisters Pauline, and Annabelle moved to Philadelphia soon after her arrival. Pansy moved to Bridgeport, Connecticut after their parents were deceased and Lofton enrolled in the military. Carla found refuge during her marital separation with Pauline. At age 31, she resolved that she would only be there until she could find employment to take care of herself. Living with her sister did not equate to having her own place but, it was a guarantee that she could be rid of Geoffrey Richards if she really wanted to be. However, he did have a hold on her as long as he had the children. You see, she did love them but it was a decision of life and death and saving her sanity. She made the only choice that she could at the time.

Carla looked for work for a week and within that time she met a very handsome, fair complexioned, heavy-set man, Harvey Kensington. She was not yet accustomed to being on her own and was not yet divorced but dared to date him for a brief time.

Periodically, she would plead with Geoffrey to see the children. She had developed the nasty habit of drinking alcohol and the last few times she visited, it was evident that she was intoxicated. Geoffrey and Carla forgot their separate living arrangements during her moments back home and found themselves making love which only seemed to leave them both in a more confused state. However, they would soon remember the hostility and anger they harbored, which instantly erased the intimacy that had just transpired between them. For years these visits ended in the bedroom. But this particular time was the beginning of another pregnancy and it caused quite a bit of turmoil in her life. Even though she was still seeing Harvey, these visits continued and when she became aware of her pregnancy she enlightened both men. She never informed Harvey of the times with Geoffrey but of course her ex-husband-to-be knew of her lover, through Pauline who would not miss an opportunity to reek havoc in her sister's life.

So, life got even more complicated for Carla. She began living with Harvey because he was willing to take care of her. But in the back of her mind she really was not sure who would end up being the father. When the baby was born, Carla came to the realization early after delivery that her son was not Harvey's and she made him aware of what had gone on behind his back. Geoffrey came to see the child and signed the birth certificate which gave little Harvey the Richards' last name. Yes, Harvey was angry at first and felt like such the fool. But, his love for her overpowered his feelings and he wanted to raise the child as his own despite the paternity. During some of her visits with her children she introduced little Harvey to them. All the Richards children understood of the situation was that they had a brother and they looked forward to their time together. Geoffrey thought that this last child would bring Carla home to stay but, to the contrary and to his surprise, she filed for divorce and went on with her life.

Carla did not love Harvey and could not fathom staying with him. So, she returned to her sister Pauline's for shelter once again. She had her newborn with her and she was determined to try to support at least one of her children. She found a job as a cook working with Stouffer's Restaurant on the outside of the city limits. She was excited because it was her first job and even though it did not pay much, it was her own money. She would take little Harvey to spend the weekends with his sisters and brothers to ensure childcare during her long hard hours on Saturdays and Sundays.

One day while waiting for the trolley, Carla met a 6 ft., fair complexioned, tall, well dressed man with wavy hair who was driving by in his shiny new blue truck. Joseph Ulzler was stalked by all kinds of women on just about every street corner. And as she noticed how attractive he was, she refused to chase but to be chased. That was the only way she had known. Oh, she was extremely interested and attracted to him but she played hard to get; no, she tried her very best to ignore him. Her scheme worked almost immediately because he noticed how Carla was not only beautiful but different from all the rest of the women he had become acquainted with. He was smitten. He offered her a ride to her destination and they began to talk. Each day afterward, Joseph offered to play taxi driver for Carla just to insure that he would see her again.

A couple of months rolled by. The relationship progressed much too rapidly for a woman who had not yet become accustomed to being on her own or settled things in her mind about her family. Never the less, Carla stopped working, moved in with Joseph and played mother to his ten children whose mother had left them to save herself.

Now, you can call it a twist of fate or just plain irony. She left behind six children to take care of one of her own and ten of a stranger. Joseph had already had two wives. One wife had ten children and left. Those ten were now grown and on their own or had run away to care for themselves. And the second wife had ten children and she opted to leave for a better life. Then there was evidence of at least three more children fathered by Joseph outside of those two marriages. Carla cared for the ten children of the last wife along with Harvey and she grew to love the Ulzler children quickly. To Carla's surprise, Joseph exceeded the violence and jealousy of Geoffrey. He also verbally and physically abused the children which explained why they were so afraid of their father and tried to stay out of his way as much as possible. He would much rather back hand one of them than show any attention or affection.

They often received the same abuse from his mother, Elvena, who did not like taking a back seat after she had assumed the mother role for the kids when their mother departed. She was known for feeding them one course meals of sticky rice and breakfast consisting of lumpy grits with no eggs or meat. The money that was given to her for food for the children was used for her gambling habit. Now, with Carla handling the money and the cooking, Elvena had less to play with. The children were convinced that her wickedness came from being a current day witch although that had never been proven.

Carolina was the meanest of Joseph's children, possibly because she was the youngest from the second marriage or she imitated the personality of Elvena and her father. No one was ever sure of what kept Carolina in such a fowl mood. After a while, everyone just ignored her. But in the years to come everyone would be in for a shock. She managed to become unimaginably more unbearable! Carla found herself trying much too hard to reach her and that irritated Carolina just about to the point of insanity. She did not like Carla or anyone for that matter. She never had much attention from anyone and the constant care from Carla made her absolutely crazy. Or was the life that those children were brought into more than they could possibly pray to survive through?

Little Harvey was brought into Joseph Ulzler's household as a very unwanted child, especially when everyone (including Joseph) viewed him as just another mouth to feed. He was beaten by the Ulzler children every opportunity that presented itself. On Carla's visits with her children, she would take Harvey along to insure his safety and he really found his brothers and sisters to be more accepting and kind than the children he lived with on a daily basis. Just from looking at him, the Richards children and their father had no doubt he belonged with them and that made each one love him that much more. The overwhelming affection from his siblings caused hatred for the children whom he had to continue to reside with if he wanted to remain with his mother. But, that posed another problem all together because he then voiced frequently how very much he wanted to be with his dad. Some time passed, then Geoffrey blatantly demanded that his child be brought home.

Carla did not put up a fight about Little Harvey because deep in her heart she knew that he was not living in the type of environment a child could be happy in, and she also knew that he was much safer with his father. Little Harvey felt terrible about choosing to live away from his mother but the pain associated with being with her and to know that she did not want to return home with him forced him to make an extremely difficult and painful decision. He arrived at the Richards' home with all of his belongings. It felt comfortable and he no longer had to fear even when his mother was not present to protect him.

Back at the Ulzler house, the fights, arguments and unwelcome wars were fought continuously for the next two years. Carla had made up in her mind that relationships were just meant to be that way. She still drank alcohol to the point of extreme intoxication and she had even managed to pick up the habit of card gambling from Joseph and his mother. Those card parties would almost always erupt into some sort of disturbance and she seemed comfortable in those situations which stemmed from her early childhood experiences. She also had come to the conclusion that if she left Joseph and someday found someone new, that relationship too would be the same because that's the way love goes. He was extreme with his jealousy though. He insisted that she stare straight ahead if they were out in a bar together just so that he could be sure she was not soliciting the attention of other men. If she even looked at the bartender straight in the eye as she ordered, Joseph would slap her right there in front of everyone. She definitely disliked the way he treated her but, there were no better alternatives in her mind. The option of being on her own and alone was not an appealing one for her at all.

CHAPTER 3

L ittle Harvey had returned home to his father's from spending the weekend with Carla. But, this time he brought back with him memories that plagued his young six year old mind. The next time Carla went to pick him up for the weekend he cried and refused to go. On the previous visit, she knew that her leaving him while she shopped, was not a good idea but he insisted. Now, she feared something happened to her child that she would never be able to make up for. When she sat down with him and inquired as to why he did not want to visit her anymore, he told her a horrid tale. She refused to believe it. She insisted that his young mind had misinterpreted or manipulated what his ears heard and his eyes witnessed.

Carla continued the love she showed to Joseph's children. She especially drew close to Lena, the oldest girl of the ten children who remained there. Lena was a beautiful 14 year old with flawless caramel skin and long wavy hair. She was shapely for her age and was lady-like in all her mannerisms. Carla and Lena had long talks which could have easily been mistaken as a mother-daughter relationship to someone with no knowledge of either of them. And Lena's questions were confided in Carla because she had assumed the role as mother to this young girl. Her own daughter, Geofreda would have been envious. But, Lena became increasingly withdrawn and refused to talk to anyone and their communications changed drastically. Carla noticed immediately and mentioned to Joseph her concerns. Of course, he did not share her feelings and merely brushed it off as, "girl stuff."

"Joseph, something is wrong with Lena lately. For the past three days I have watched her mope around and she is so quiet," Carla expressed.

"What the hell do you expect me to do? You are the damn girl's mother. You figure it out!" Joseph shouted as he stomped out of the room and down the stairs of the two-story dwelling. He was headed for Pep Boys where he worked as a mechanic.

Carla continued to watch Lena for a few more days and when the overall demeanor of the child did not change, she went to her. "Lena, baby, what's wrong with you lately? I've been watching and something is bothering you. Tell me what it is?" Carla pleaded.

Lena looked into Carla's eyes and knew that she was the only person who would at least be willing to help her. As tears streamed down her face, she explained to her common-law stepmother what ate away at her heart.

Little Harvey was there for the weekend and she watched him while she waited for Carla and Joseph to return from grocery shopping and paying bills. Lena loved Harvey and was always the only one that really cared for him. She was teaching him how to play jacks and his interest in the game took precedence over everything else because he forgot about the potential dangers he would be in if he did not remain by his mother's side. Consequently, he was not the one in danger that time.

All the other children were either outside in the backyard playing or out front on the steps of the house as they had been instructed by the oldest, Ross. Marcus (age 15) and Ross (age 16), chased Lena around every inch of the house as soon as the adults turned the corner for their destination. She was pursued from room to room upstairs until she was too exhausted and drained of energy to run any farther. There in the small room, Ross and Marcus pushed her down onto the floor and worked as a team to complete the plan they had plotted for months. Ross removed her panties and then tied her hands to the foot of the bed. He spread her legs slightly apart and sat on her feet and ankles to immobilize her as he faced away from Lena. Marcus pulled up her dress so that it covered her face and sucked one of her innocent breasts while he removed his pants and under-wear which exposed his true intentions. He then straddled his sister, which placed him back to back with Ross, and penetrated her virgin body with his. She screamed and cried. No one came to her aid. But, someone did hear her plea for help. Harvey witnessed the entire thing from the doorway of an adjacent room and was petrified.

"Oh, God!" she cried. "You're hurting me! Get off of me!"

She did not know what was more painful, the hard floor against her head, the weight of her brothers on her frail back, buttocks and ankles; the tight rope around her wrists or her vagina which seemed as though it was being ripped out of her with every forceful stroke. As soon as Marcus finished with her and the sound of her hoarse screams could barely be heard, Ross took his turn. He too engaged in intercourse with his sister.

"You'd better not say nothin' about this, girl! You think you're hurting now? I'll show you," Ross threatened. He untied her and left her sitting there sobbing. Ross and Marcus giggled to themselves how good it felt to have sex. And now that they had easy access to it; they planned more of the same. After five or ten minutes, Ross returned to the room and made her clean up the blood and sweat. He threatened her with even more intense consequences if she verbalized the events to a single soul.

Carla was appalled and could find no words to console the trembling victim who looked to her for relief. She took Lena into her arms and rocked her back and forth like a small child that had been wounded by mad dogs. Immediately, a piercing thought came to mind which prompted her to ask a question.

"Lena, do you know what a menstrual cycle is?"

"Yes," she answered in bewilderment.

"Do you have yours yet?"

"No, I don't have mine yet," she quickly responded.

"Thank God!" Carla sighed.

She was so relieved to find Lena was not menstruating and there was no chance of an incestuous pregnancy. Lena was able to convince her not to approach the boys because she actually feared what her brothers would do to her and pleaded that the ugly incident be buried and forgotten. She knew that her father had the compassion of an alley cat and really would make more trouble than it was worth. But the older and wiser woman insisted on at least informing Joseph. The young teen aired all of the dirty laundry and it had proven therapeutic. Just to have shared and talked with her confidant about the ordeal made the sight of her brothers somewhat more tolerable.

Thoughts of Harvey's behavior flashed through Carla's mind after talking with Lena. His demeanor on the day she went to pick him up for the weekend now made sense. Ironically, he corroborated Lena's story even before it was told and it was true. The whole ugly tale was very true and not merely a misconstrued notion of a six year old as Carla first believed. She never talked about it again with Harvey though. She believed that he was better off uncertain of what he witnessed which left a trail of confusion in his mind that he struggled to overcome later in life.

At approximately 1:30 a.m. on Monday morning, after Harvey's refusal to come for the weekend, Carla told Joseph about the rapes that took place. He simply refused to believe it.

"You are a God-damned liar!" he shouted as he jumped out of bed. "That shit never happened! You're a damned liar!" he repeated.

He flung the door open to their bedroom and stormed into the room that Lena shared with three of her sisters. He snatched her out of a sound sleep, grabbed her by the arm and literally drug her to his bedroom where Carla was sitting up in shock. He slammed the door behind him and slung Lena onto the bed which finally released the vice-grip he held on her arm since removing her from her bed.

"What's this shit about your brothers? Huh? What the fuck is going on?"

When Lena was finally coherent and realized what her father was so angry about, she looked at him with intense fear. But, she stood up and relived the events surrounding the extremely painful experience. Before she was completely finished her father lunged to slap her face but, Carla was able to quickly and strategically place herself between Joseph and the child.

"You little bitch! You made them want you! You're always prissin' around here. They are young boys that have needs and you know good and well you liked it. You loved every minute of what they did. You've been wanting it for a long time!" Joseph was furious and his tone of voice left no doubt about it.

Lena sat down on the edge of the bed and sobbed hysterically. Joseph grabbed his pants and shirt that were flung across the back of a chair, his shoes and truck keys and stormed out of the house. Carla held and caressed Lena's head tight to her bosom until she stopped crying. For quite some time neither of them spoke and the quiet that filled the room seemingly magnified Lena's heartbeat which seemed audible from every corner. The rest of the house was still sound asleep. No one stirred to get out of bed or even listen to the late night commotion because of the frequency of fights.

"I'm sorry I made you tell your father about this. You were right to say that it was better off forgotten. Baby, I'm so very sorry!" Carla softly spoke into her ear.

Lena didn't respond. As far as she was concerned, her lapse in memory began the moment of her father's irrational verbal attack. In time, the scars of the rapes would be partially healed and buried but never forgotten by Lena, Harvey or Carla.

Carla found herself pregnant again at age 39. She was devastated to know that one of her own children would have to endure the cold and calculating ways of a father such as Joseph. What little respect she did possess for him diminished when he reacted in the manner in which he did when he was told of the rapes. Usually, when a woman is found with child, immediately her mind is resolved that she must take extra care of herself for the child's sake. Carla really did not want the baby and her normal behaviors of drinking, gambling, fighting and cursing never ceased. The lifestyle was truly in her blood. She prayed for a miscarriage religiously but no matter what was done, the pregnancy continued much to Carla's dismay. At six and a half months, Carla went into labor and was taken to Temple University Hospital to deliver. Joseph lied on the admissions paperwork and gave his companion's name as Carla Ulzler even though they had not so much as discussed marriage. His motive was to give the child his last name because Carla still carried her ex-husband's. The child was granted his last name not because Joseph cared but it was attributed to his huge ego.

"My child will not carry another man's name," he thought to himself.

Delivery lasted only a few hours in comparison to her previous ones and the fruit of her labor was a still born son. He had died days prior but she never stopped long enough to notice there was no movement. She named the boy Reynold only at the encouragement of the nurses and left the disposal of the child up to the hospital because they did not desire a memorial service. No show of emotion, no regrets, no remorse........nothing.

There was very little mention of the son that never came home from the hospital that night. The children were never told of the existence of the pregnancy and Joseph had just gained knowledge himself when Carla was already five months. It was an easy concealment. She had just begun to show a little when Reynold was born/died. The only evidence of his little life was the birth certificate with his name, birth date, parents, weight, length and the words "still born" written by hand at the bottom. This document was stuffed away with other important papers, pictures and memoirs in an old purse which would later be referred to as "the bag of secrets."

For the longest time after the loss of Reynold, Carla refused to allow Joseph to even kiss her. As hard of a life as it already was, the fights became more brutal. Joseph's sexual frustration and an inner turmoil within Carla made the little row house on Sergeant Street a daily war zone. Joseph drank and gambled increasingly and his job immediately suffered. He rarely reported for work and when he did grace Pep Boys with his presence, he was terribly late and intoxicated. Because he had been one of their finest employees, the company tried to work with him and hoped against hope that it was just a stage he was going through. He was reprimanded for cursing other employees and customers and he was suspended several times for verbally and physically assaulting his immediate supervisor among other violations. These actions were grounds for immediate termination, but his 13 year, flawless prior work record bought him more time than he deserved. Finally, after three months of unruly behavior, he was fired.

CHAPTER 4

The last thing that you would have expected, occurred on February 17, 1963. Carla gave birth to a baby girl at the age of 42. Their daughter was born two and a half months premature and weighed only 4 lbs. and 1 oz. Regina Lenette Ulzler was tiny, beautiful, healthy and alive! Carla found herself anxious when the labor pains began as she replayed Reynold's still birth over and over in her mind. Yes, she drank, gambled and fought during the pregnancy with her daughter as she had previously but, she put forth a concerted effort to insure that history did not repeat itself. When her addictions tried to overpower her sense of responsibility, she occasionally refrained by remembering Reynold's lifeless body as it was removed from her womb.

"He never cried," she said to herself and a tear streamed down her face. There was remorse after all. She felt this child's assignment was to give her another chance to somehow vindicate herself from how she and Joseph grossly mishandled their son and his death.

Carla and Joseph had been together now approximately four years and still had not married. Therefore, Joseph again gave the hospital the impression that he and Carla were husband and wife. He did not want it to be an obvious advertisement that Regina was his bastard child. The effort was futile however. Even though she was gifted or cursed with the Ulzler last name, Regina still grew up feeling like a bastard; she never sensed that she belonged anywhere.

Because she was so little, Carla had to leave Regina in Temple University Hospital for two weeks. She could not be discharged until she weighed at least 5 lbs. When Carla visited, she always found Regina being held by someone, a doctor or a nurse from either of the shifts rocked and talked to her. Because she was completely bald except for one small strand of hair in the top of her head, they habitually rubbed it as if a powerful magnetic force automatically drew their hand to it.

"She was born a member of the bald eagle club," they joked.

"Well, I came to take the little eagle to her nest today," Carla replied and smiled.

As she stood in the elevator leaving the hospital for home, she thought back to when she brought Harvey to the Ulzler home to live. She could only hope that Regina, being one of them, would be accepted and loved. But how could those children show emotions that had never truly been shown as an example for them? All they were accustomed to was violence and anger and unfortunately that was exactly how the innocent child was received.

Joseph's twin girls, Cora and Dora were the only ones that took an interest in Regina. To them, she served as a life-sized baby doll and they pretended to care for her in the manner in which they would have desired to have been as an infant. All the others saw her as a nuisance. Furthermore, the small frail infant required much more attention than anyone other than the twins were willing to invest. Carla felt that she had done her duty when she sacrificed her habits periodically for a healthy baby and immediately plunged full force back into her vicious destructive cycle.

Regina was approximately 18 months old and still found it difficult to keep her balance. The high top, hard bottom shoes provided some stability. But, she heard a loud noise and turned quickly in the direction of the sound. Five year old Carolina was sitting on the sofa within reach and Regina grabbed her leg with both hands to avoid falling. As she made contact with Carolina, her sharp little fingernails unintentionally scratched her sibling. Next, the toddler felt extreme pain across her chubby right cheek and the hard linoleum floor onto which she fell. Carolina struck her with all her might and the incident remained etched in Regina's mind as one of her earliest memories.

Subsequently, as most children who are insecure about their surroundings develop habits; Regina became quite attached to her right thumb. She tried the left one but, it just did not appease her at all. Carla did not spend very much time with her. Therefore, one of the twins brought it to her attention that Regina could not be stopped from sucking her thumb at night and the intoxicated mother was prompted to wrap up the finger with a rag that she had torn from an old dress. She tied the cloth in a tight knot and then nailed the excess to the wall beside the bed. Of course, the act of abuse caused the child to be extremely irritable which was not her usual demeanor. She cried for over half the night. She drifted off to sleep for a brief period just to be awakened a short while later by the struggle to free her right hand. Dora had mercy and released the finger from its prison and remained watchful to remove it gently from her sister's mouth if she managed to find her friend, "Mr. Thumb." During the day, Carla placed iodine on it so that the bitter taste discouraged sucking and instead it encouraged the toddlers lips to swell. But for Regina, the thumb merely served as her hero and a little piece of comfort in an extremely uncomfortable place called life.

At two and a half years of age, Regina witnessed a terrible altercation between her mother and grandmother. The two were playing poker one evening and Elvena won every single one of the eight straight games that were played. Carla accused her of cheating. A heated argument with both women cursing like sailors was the beginning of a battle with vicious blows thrown. Even though Carla used profanity, she used it in general. She never called Elvena other than her name. But when Joseph's mother called her a "money hungry Bitch," Carla climbed across the long, heavy oak table where she sat directly in front of her opponent. One minute she had cards in hand and within seconds, she was crouched on her knees on the table top, eyes full of rage as she choked the life from her verbal attacker. Not even Regina's cries could distract her attention from the focus on fighting. The assault lasted well over 30 minutes and ended at 1:45 a.m. when Joseph quickly stepped in to play referee after he returned from a long adventure of his own.

Joseph soon let alcohol consume his every thought and the majority of his time. Since fired from Pep Boys, he worked here and there. But he never stayed anywhere for more than a month. He always came home with reason not to go back and used that as an excuse for alcohol consumption. Of course, the finances digressed into a terrible state. Candles replaced electricity, a hot plate replaced the stove when money was found to turn the electricity back on. Water was heated on the hot plate for bathing and the fireplace in the living room downstairs served as the only source of heat for the entire dwelling. For what little food there was, the refrigerator was replaced by a tightly packed cooler filled with ice supplied by Elvena. Joseph's temper increased, especially when he traded the truck he owned for the automobile which suddenly became a victim of repossession. Only four payments which totaled $500.00 remained to be paid on the vehicle before the terms of the loan would have been met. It was the grace of God that kept housing from becoming a problem.

You see, Elvena and her husband had owned the house on Sergeant Street since they first married and it served as rental property after the house was paid-in-full years prior. Joseph paid his rent on time and never took advantage of the fact that his landlords just so happened to be his parents. But, when he fell upon hard times and there was no job to pay the $120.00 per month, Joseph was lucky that the roof over his head was provided through Elvena and she graciously opted for the loss of income to accommodate her favorite child in his time of need. The only responsibilities left to him regarding the house was the utilities and the upkeep which he lacked the initiative to do successfully. He did not see alcohol and gambling as the root of the downward spiral in life. But, it definitely was. He viewed life as just some cruel game that he lost every now and then and his addictions were to soften the punches that lady luck had thrown his way. He had no idea of what caused the repossession of his vehicle. He was clueless as to why he had lost his job. He never even stopped long enough to care about how to regain his possessions or the opportunity to reverse his sudden misfortune.

Of course Carla found herself unable to depend on Joseph for basic necessities such as food and warmth. Sadly, he could no longer provided fuel for her warped lifestyle and her so called love for him took flight. The money was gone. The security had disappeared. The basic essentials were now non-existent. All

the common-law husband had to offer now was violence, suffering, and indig-
nation and she faced the reality that she finally had to obtain independence. Even
his good looks faded and suffered momentary lapses because he was seldom
sober enough to be considered handsome. She had to become self-sufficient,
relying solely on her own ability to take care of herself and her child. She would
not be made to do without ever again because someone else failed or refused to
provide.

Carla's solution was to visit an old friend who lived at 2509 Popular Street
and asked for shelter until she could be gainfully employed and recovered from
her stormy life with Joseph. She was able to walk there because it was only five
or six blocks from where she currently resided. Hanna McDuffie had become her
friend during one of the numerous card parties and drinking sessions that Harvey
Kensington had introduced her to. She went in hopes of finding shelter with the
acquaintance who affectionately called her "Crimpy Top." The name referred to
her large naturally wavy locks of hair. Carla explained the living conditions in
which she had allowed herself to become engulfed. Hanna offered her home
openly without coercion and before her distressed friend had a chance to make
her request known. So, without so much as a word to anyone and no explanation,
she left Joseph just as she had Geoffrey. She packed only clothing for herself and
Regina and started her new life.

Hanna was a fair complexioned, short, heavy-set woman with long gray hair
and a glass right eye. Her worst habit was her nasty compulsion to dip snuff. She
stopped card gambling which encouraged Carla's decreased efforts to participate
in the games as well. Hanna had replaced risky stakes with running a number
house where she also sold liquor. Her 11 year old grand-daughter, Tangy, lived
with her. Amazingly, she and Regina became bosom buddies even though Tangy
preceded her in age by six years. Regina stayed with Hanna daily as Carla
regained her job at Stouffer's. She had only been employed there two months
before she terminated her work status with the major restaurant chain but her
culinary skills were superb.

Her supervisor once commented, "It is not only a natural gift that you hold;
it is a gift from God. Everything you concoct seems like a little piece of heaven."

She customarily prepared only soul food when she first accepted the chef
position. But, she found it easy to follow the recipes and mastered the art of pres-
entation from the pictures in the cook books. The dishes she had no knowledge
of prior to employment, became her specialties.

With her success as a cook came confidence to move out on her own. She
had managed to save enough money to rent a small furnished, inexpensive, run-
down, two room apartment she found on 10th Street, ten blocks away from
Hanna. The three-story house had been divided/converted into apartments; each
level housed two apartments and a centrally located, semi-public bathroom. The
lavatory that had to be shared with the perfect strangers who were occupants of
her second floor and the mandatory distance away from her place made Carla

leery. Her corner front apartment faced 10th Street. It had two entrances; one from the kitchen and the other from the room that served as a bedroom/living room combination. The kitchen had a refrigerator, stove, sink, and a dinette. Three dead bolt locks were strategically placed on the inside of that door so as to eliminate potential access for would-be burglars. Carla bought a small cot to serve as Regina's bed and placed it by the wall adjacent to the bedroom/living room which purposely obstructed the heavily secured kitchen passageway. The monstrous second room consisted of a full sized bed, a night stand, a large chest (at the foot of the bed), a dresser, a sofa and two single chairs. None of the furnishings were in good condition but that was of no major concern. Carla and Regina could finally live without alcohol and violence, in peace.

Carla worked days initially but after six months or so, she was placed on the evening shift. She disliked it because her childcare needs would be forced to change. Hanna would have to supervise Regina day and night and Carla preferred such a responsibility to fall on a family member. Because she was Stouffer's best cook, management compromised with Carla in hopes to relieve some of her parenting pressure; they granted weekends off to compensate for her inconvenience. She did not know how to drive and relied on SEPTA, the city public transit system, to travel to and from work. By the time her shift was over at 11:00 p.m., her station cleaned and next day meal preparation finished, she then traveled two buses, a train and a trolley home. She arrived daily at 3:00 a.m. exhausted and good for nothing but sleep. Carla felt the hours that were required of her hindered proper ability to care for the needs of her daughter so she arranged with her sister, Pauline, for Regina to live with her during the week and spend weekends at home.

On off days Carla slept, which left Regina to entertain herself. She was provided with coloring books, crayons, paper and an old second hand TV which Carla had purchased on credit. She had never needed a loan for anything because someone had always been responsible for her. The old black and white TV was placed in the corner of the bedroom/living room and Carla was quite proud of her first possession. Yes, times were hard. But, the southern girl had mastered the great art of budgeting from the days when Geoffrey gave her the money to run their household and she would squeeze movie money from it without creating shortages in any other area of the finances. If he gave her money to feed the eight of them, she always had money left over. She was known for stretching a dollar like rubber.......a long, long way.

CHAPTER 5

Things appeared to be good for Carla and she exhibited pride about what she had managed to accomplish on her own. Then one day, Frank Barker waltzed into her life as she prepared to leave work. He had been in the restaurant for the majority of the evening eating. From the salad through desert took him, a record breaking four hours and five minutes which seemed odd for a man who dined alone with no one in which to hold conversation. The waitress assigned to his table was courteous and extremely expedient in taking his requests and in delivery of the food. So, untimely, poor service was not the guilty culprit for his prolonged meal. She had never witnessed anyone eat as slowly as he did that night but Barker had a motive for savoring every bite. Not only was the scrumptious food delightful to his palate, he had managed to lay eyes on the chef and was engrossed by her beauty. His determination to meet her prompted the Guinness World Record attempt (for slowest eater).

She first felt his gaze from across the restaurant. Several times their eyes met and each encounter left her enchanted by the pleasant smile he so comfortably displayed on his face. He was tall, pecan complexioned, heavy-set but well proportioned with beautiful hazel eyes and fine, wavy hair. Every strand was combed back strategically to expose his handsome features. He was impeccably dressed and his costly clothes and cologne made it obviously evident that he had exceptional taste. His gold watch and black onyx ring added that special finish which added a distinguished look as though he was worth more than a million bucks. As attractive as he was though, he had one flaw. He believed that he could have any woman that he wanted. His money, fine possessions and cars were his insurance. Unfortunately for him, arrogance was the one thing that Carla hated most in a man.

She returned smiles to Barker all night and it became clear after a while that he ingested slowly for an opportunity to meet her. Near the end of her shift, she boldly approached his table.

"You look like you really enjoyed yourself tonight?"

"I did," he admitted.

"What is your name?" she inquired.

"Barker."

" My name is Carla. How was your meal?"

"I don't know. I haven't finished yet. I believe I may have another desert," he replied as he looked at her as if she was something good to eat.

"Well Barker, you'll need to hurry and decide on that desert because we close in ten minutes," she said as she smiled at his flirtatious comment and slipped him a folded piece of paper.

"My shift is over at 11:00 and it takes an hour to close up my station."

She walked away and glanced back at the handsome stranger over her left shoulder. He blushed as he read her message. He then left the waitress a hefty tip and waited outside in front with anticipation to meet the author of his note. It was cold and 2' of snow was on the ground. Barker exited his car just in time to open the door of the restaurant for Carla's departure for the night.

"Thank you," she replied to his kind show of manners.

"You are very welcome. Can I walk you to your car?" Barker asked.

She quickly explained. "I don't own one but my bus stop is only a block away."

"I insist on driving you home. It is too late for any woman to be walking alone, especially one as beautiful as you."

"He is such a gentleman. Or is it a way to spend more time with me? As cold as it is, I'm not crazy enough to turn down his offer," she thought to herself.

Carla said a quick prayer under her breath for safety and gratefully accepted the ride. Her usual travel time was two hours and forty-five minutes but he swiftly and carefully maneuvered the car through the snow covered streets to show his responsibility to see her home safely. The trip by car, was a one hour, ten minute drive. The car gracefully pulled up to her front door and came to a complete stop.

"Thank you so much for the ride and the compliments. I needed them both." Carla expressed. "How much do I owe you?"

"Your thanks paid your car fare but you can reward me with your phone number."

"She sadly replied, "I don't have one."

"No woman living alone should be without a phone. Or do you live alone?" He had interrupted before she could answer. "I guess I should have asked if you were married or had a live in boyfriend. It's a little late but, now I'm asking." He looked concerned and cautiously scoped out her windows and door for any sign of a jealous companion.

"You can relax. I live with my five year old daughter."

"In that case, I beg you to let me provide a phone for you," he pleaded.

Carla gave no response but smiled at him as she removed herself from the warm, new vehicle that smelled of its owner's cologne.

"Thank you again for everything," she said and faded behind the wooden door. The only remnant of her was her tracks in the snow.

Regina was a mild mannered and considerate child. That was the reason she was so deeply hurt by the reaction of Joseph's children when she went for visits. They first ignored her, then they hated her. The only woman that had shown them any compassion or real love was now gone and they felt that Regina was considerably more fortunate because of that fact. Unlike their mother, Carla placed her child as top priority over her quest for freedom and saved her from the heathen clutches of their dad and grandmother. In their minds, the love that they knew for Carla responsibly bound her to them as well as their sister. They resented the well combed hair and adorable outfits that now were afforded. But it was simply easier to provide for just one child. If she was to struggle to care for more, then her obligation to her biological children would never have been abandoned.

Regina was destined to experience what her brother Harvey endured. Caroline fought her as the others taunted, teased and harassed her. Regina soon despised the thought of visitation and firmly decided not to see them again. Carla was not insistent after Regina was so adamant about terminating the warped relationship and their next reunion did not take place until their grandmother Elvena's funeral years later.

The work schedule changed yet again. Carla was to work the night shift from 11:00 p.m. until 7:00 in the morning. Regina would begin Kindergarten that year. So, arrangements to have her enrolled in school in Pauline's neighborhood was set for June, even though she turned school age earlier in February. Pauline's children were in their early twenties and teens and her grandchildren were a few years younger than Regina. She loved the thought of other children to play with. She had become accustomed to the friendship of Tangy and was grateful not to have to return to loneliness.

Pauline's husband, Donald, injured himself on his job and received monthly compensation. He remained in a drunken stupor from day to day but refused to believe that he was an alcoholic. It was rumored that Pauline was so mean and hateful to him until he turned to alcohol for solace and found it more tolerable than his wife. In other words, he would much rather not know where he was than to deal with her. During the times when he was only slightly belligerent, they argued and Pauline would beat him with anything that she could grasp in her hands. Alcohol was definitely his escape.

Pauline's 15 year old, Dena, showered her young cousin with attention and Regina automatically became attached to her. They journeyed everywhere together and she shared money, treats and a large portion of her time. After just a short while, she was promoted in Regina's heart as her favorite cousin because nothing pleased the naive one more than warm acceptance. They took walks to watch Dena's sister, Bonnie, assassinate all the boys in basketball. They played many fun games........hide and seek, monster, jump rope and jacks just to name a few.

But that evening after dinner, Dena told Regina, "We are gonna play a secret game later tonight. No one else can play. It will be something special only the two of us will know about. I can't tell anyone else but you," Dena proudly boasted.

Regina was overcome with anticipation regarding the new game that her preferred cousin was going to introduce to her. She tried her best to stay awake until the appointed time but she had been programmed to surrender to sleep by 10:00 p.m. The droopy brown eyes tried their best not to comply with the general bedtime rule but the clock read 11:30, and her fight with the inevitable was over. She fell fast asleep in Dena's bed as she did every night. At 1:45 a.m., Dena woke Regina from a sound sleep.

"It's time for our secret game."

"Oh goody!" Regina said in a sleepy tone of voice as she rubbed her eyes and struggled against her body's attempts to remain semi-conscious.

There were two sisters sleeping in the beds closest to the entrance and Dena looked over toward them as she closed the door to the bedroom. Only the dim lamp on the night stand gave light. She motioned to the child to keep very quiet so as not to awaken the others.

"Step on the bed and sit on top of the dresser," Dena instructed.

"What's the name of this game?" The youngster was very anxious.

"We are going to play doctor. You will be the patient and I will be the doctor," Dena said. "Now, take off your panties and open your legs."

"Why do I have to take my panties off? Can't we play with them on?" Regina already felt extremely uncomfortable with the game.

"I thought we were best friends? If we are, you'll just do like I say," Dena encouraged. Regina no longer wanted to play the game but she could not bear the thought of losing the one cousin who had treated her so kindly. So, reluctantly she removed her underpants.

"Now, open your legs wide. It's time to look at you. Be real quiet." Dena continued to guard against any noise that would wake potential witnesses to her crime. She had no knowledge of proper doctor technique and ignorantly placed both her index and middle finger into Regina's body. Immediately tears streamed down her face.

"I don't like this game Dena, it hurts, I want to stop now! Please can we stop?" she sobbed.

"I thought that you were a big girl but I see you're just a baby. I'll never play with you again."

Physically and emotionally in pain, Regina returned her undergarment to its original position. She descended from the dresser by stepping back onto the foot of the bed and traveled into the bathroom a short distance down the hallway on the right. Her need to urinate was urgent and she sat on the toilet for relief but instead burned unbearably and found reason to sob with more intensity. Regina remained there on the stool for approximately an hour before she wiped away the traces of blood and urine which proved that Dena's long, strong nails had scratched the inner vagina walls and torn tissue. The weeping child went back to bed to find Dena already fast asleep. Even though the room was dark, it took Regina two additional hours before she returned to dreamland where she relived her most recent nightmare.

CHAPTER 6

Regina slept late the Saturday morning after the molestation. She was physically exhausted from lack of sleep and also emotionally drained from the toll of the night before. Everyone else in the house had risen, eaten and started their day; everyone, that is, but Donald. Regina finally awoke at 11:15 with cold which had formed in her eyes over night and both eyes were sealed completely shut. The child felt her way out of the room, down the long hall and held on to the banister as she carefully descended each stair. She could hear her mother's voice as she reached the mid-way point and began to call out to her.

"Mommy," she cried. "Something's wrong with my eyes!"

The first attempt did not gain anyone's attention and so another effort was made. This time, the sound of her child's scared voice reached Carla and she rushed toward the staircase.

"What's the matter?" she asked as she looked into her daughter's face. She could see the yellow mucus that had dried though the small lashes.

"Pauline, get me a hot, damp cloth. Regina's got cold in her eyes and she can't see."

When her request was granted, Carla worked for quite some time to get the eyes freed from their entrapment. One eye was unglued within the first five minutes and it took an additional seven minutes for the second. Regina had been fighting with a terrible cold for the past week and Carla did not find the condition of her eyes anything to become alarmed about.

"Regina, are you hungry? There is a little breakfast left over," said Pauline's oldest daughter, Clarese.

"No, I'm not hungry," replied the child in a faint weak voice. She clung to her mother's side. Carla led Regina into the living room and seated themselves across from Pauline. Clarese, Bonnie, Betsy, Deitra, Gerline and her boyfriend were watching cartoons in the living room while their mother and Carla talked about documents necessary to enroll Regina in school. Dena had gone shopping with a friend an hour or so prior.

Carla noticed that Regina was extremely quiet and not herself. Even though no one really paid too much attention to her and she never held many conversations, it was obvious that her behavior was strange. Carla's work schedule had Regina quite accustomed to keeping herself busy. She usually played with her Barbie dolls. She would often talk aloud while pretending with them and was completely independent. Instead, today she sat close by Carla's side which was a clue that something was terribly wrong.

"Does your cold have you feeling bad?"

"I'm OK," the child responded in the same faint voice as before.

"Well, what's wrong with you. And don't tell me nothing!" Carla was convinced something was not right with her daughter.

"Dena made me play doctor last night and it hurts," she explained. "It still hurts."

"What still hurts? Where do you hurt?" Her mother became really interested and the tone of her voice made everyone in the room take notice of the conversation.

Regina's small index finger pointed between her legs, directly above her vaginal area. Alarm swept over Carla and her heart pounded hard enough to leap completely from her chest. After the entire epic was told, a family feud broke out. Everyone had a comment to make.

" I don't believe it!" Pauline yelled. "I sure as hell don't believe it!"

"She's lying," yelled Clarese!

"What would make you say such a thing, Regina?" Bonnie managed to squeeze out enough wind to ask. Her breath had been taken away.

"Where is Dena?" Clarese directed the question to Pauline.

"She's not here but, Regina is nothing but a little liar!"

"I know it's hard to believe Ma," Gerline reasoned. "But there are too many details to just ignore it."

"I'm not going to sit here and let some little bastard lie on my baby girl in my house..... in my face!" Pauline's temper was about to erupt. "That's about all I can take of this! Get the hell out of my house right now! This shit is ridiculous! Get her out of here Carla, I mean it! You'd better get her ass out of here!"

Stunned and overwhelmed, Carla collected Regina's things together and removed herself. She and her daughter said nothing the entire bus and trolley trip home. But because Regina kept complaining of pain, Carla sought the services of the local clinic and had her examined on the following Monday after the sexual abuse.

"Why don't you explain to me why you are here to see me?" the doctor said to Regina through a half-cocked smile.

The traumatized child remembered the chaos of the last time she told of Friday night and began to cry. Dena's actions had done enormous damage but, the family's reaction was just as devastating.

"Regina, you've got to tell the doctor what happened so he can help you. If you don't, he may not be able to make you feel better," her mother explained.

As she began to relive all that took place during the weekend, she periodically had to stop and catch her breath from crying. She was already tired of talking about it and just wanted to forget that it had ever happened. However, each time she urinated reminded her and she vividly envisioned the red brightly polished fingernails drawing nearer to her to inflict injury.

The Caucasian man, with the salt and pepper hair and beard, listened intently. When he heard the accounts of the ordeal, he was saddened by its need to be told. Of course, he regretfully found it necessary to examine for evidence of the alleged incident.

"No! I don't want anybody to go down there. It hurts! It hurts!" Regina screamed.

Even though the doctor sympathized, "Regina we must see what is wrong. I'll be real careful and I will try my best not to hurt you. But, I can't help you if you won't let me."

"Nooooo!!!!!" She was stiff with anxiety as the exam proceeded.

"Mrs. Ulzler, I could see the irritation that is causing the pain during urination and the irritation is conducive with what your daughter said. I also apologize for my having to report this to the Department of Welfare for Children."

"Oh, God, I don't want those people all in my life. I have enough to deal with," Carla pleaded. "I didn't do this to her and it didn't happen where we live. Her cousin where I leave her while I work nights did this. I'll quit my job, I'll get another one; anything to keep from risking her from being hurt again. I'll stay home with her myself and I'll never let her go over there again. Doctor, do you really have to report this? Please for God sake, I feel guilty enough for trusting her around teen-agers! I beg you, don't report it? I don't want to risk my daughter being taken from me."

He examined her facial expression and body language. "I have your word that she will not be left in that home again?" The doctor looked at Carla with inquisitive and searching eyes.

Carla also explained the turmoil that followed after Regina notified the family of Dena's behavior. "I assure you we are no longer welcome at my sister's house."

Satisfied with the impression that he received from Carla's stressed face, he closed the file and returned his pen to his clinical jacket pocket. "For the record then, my diagnosis is a possible bladder infection. It is imperative that she drink large quantities of water and just in case there is some infection, I want to give her an antibiotic. The pain should go away as the irritation dissipates. That's all I can do. But, if things worsen you must bring her back to me. May God bless you and your daughter, Mrs. Ulzler."

CHAPTER 7

C arla found the truth during the doctor's visit that day. But, even though there was no doubt about what transpired between Dena and Regina, Carla promised her daughter she would never have to talk about it again. It had inflicted enough damage and the family would never be the same because of it. So, this was another family secret to be forgotten and then to eventually become nonexistent in memory. Regina was not sure whether her mother told anyone. But, she knew some excuse was provided to her Aunt Annabelle as a reason for need for childcare. Carla asked her sister to care for the youngster until she could make better arrangements regarding work.

Annabelle and her husband Justin had four teenage children and they shared a good family life. Justin insisted that Annabelle not work. He wanted to be the sole provider for his family. He was a hard worker and was known for his many trades and managed to primarily work for himself. But, he was best known for the enormous love he possessed for Annabelle. She wanted for nothing and whatever she desired, he happily worked twice as hard to get it for her. She was showered with the very best that life could offer and strangely, there was no major drama in that household or for her brother, Lofton. It seemed as though only the two of them had escaped the family curse. Maybe Annabelle and Lofton were too young to remember when the other siblings witnessed the violence of their parents. Or were they too masters at abiding by the family rule? "What goes on in this house, stays in this house." Only God knew the answer to that question. Either way, her family appeared well adjusted and happy.

Regina found her aunt to be a kind-natured and loving person. She loved to follow her around the house watching her do what she loved most, cook. Her excessively heavy-set body was evidence of her favorite pastime.

Annabelle's sons, Ralph age 13 and Justin Jr. age 15, were both instructed in the martial arts. Every lesson day, they would come home and practice the techniques they had learned on Regina in the basement. It was all done in fun though and no ill was intended. However, Regina grew tired of being flipped around like a rag doll and closely paid attention to their movements. She did not know or even understand the terms they used, but she imitated them and found that she was exceptionally good at faking it. She did not realize that the fun she found generated her toughness and she gained skills that she later utilized to protect herself. One afternoon when Ralph looked for his cousin to spar with, he was unsuccessful. She had hidden herself from him. Before she could be located, she jumped out at him and showcased her new found talent. He was so astonished at her abilities until he was caught off guard and taken to the floor by a five year old. She bragged to everyone in the house. Annabelle's youngest daughter, Brenda, could hear Regina shout all the way upstairs where she watched TV.

"I knocked Ralph down! I knocked him down on the floor with Karate! I know Karate!" she yelled to anyone who would listen. Ralph on the other hand surfaced from the basement a little embarrassed and still in a state of shock. He insisted that she tripped him when he was not looking.

Carla continued to work at Stouffer's. The same routine that was kept with Pauline was also followed with Annabelle. Regina was retrieved every Saturday morning to spend the weekend at home. During the first summer on 10th Street, Carla allowed Regina to go outside to sit on the front steps to play. She was not allowed to move from directly in front of the house and there she sat and played with her paper dolls and Barbies. She looked to her left and directly next door there was a young ten year old girl playing jacks on her front steps. The two of them eyed each other for a while and soon the neighbor broke into conversation.

"Hey, what's your name little girl?"

"Regina."

"Why don't you come over here and play with me?"

"I can't. My mom said I can only sit on the steps."

"Well, then go ask her can you come over."

Regina collected her dolls and went upstairs to the second floor. "Mom, can I sit on the steps next door? There is a girl over there and she asked me could I come over and play with her."

Carla peered out of the window down to the street below to see who Regina spoke of. There sat a young girl totally engrossed in her game of jacks. Carla gave her permission but instructed the eager child not to go any further than the adjacent house. Before the words were finished, Regina was already down the hall and near the long staircase.

"Remember, don't go any further and don't go inside nobody's house!" Carla yelled.

The child had already made it to the front door headed toward a new friend-ship. Darla was her name. One of her eyes was crossed and children that passed by called her "cock-eyed". Yes, she appeared different. She also sucked both her index and middle finger simultaneously until saliva ran down the back of her hand to her elbow. But, none of that mattered to Regina because she knew what it felt like to be different and teased. She refused to be judgmental of her new friend just because she was different. All she knew was that Darla liked playing with her and the feeling was mutual. Regina and Darla played for hours at a time. They never argued. They never misbehaved. They just enjoyed each others company which made life for both a great deal easier.

Playing with Darla became a daily ritual when Regina was home. On this particular day though, some youth with bad reputations started teasing Darla which made the both of them very uncomfortable. Darla's grandmother, Lela Whitfield, was watching from her wheelchair which was positioned in front of the window but out of plain view. In anticipation of trouble she came to the door to detour any bad conduct. The gross attitudes of the strangers made her so uneasy until she urged both girls to retreat inside the house.

"I can't come in," said Regina. "My mother told me that I can't go in anyone's house. I'll get a whipping if I do."

"These kids are up to no good, get in here where it's safe," she urged as the young gangsters kept hurling insults at her.

Darla had already taken refuge and stood behind her grandmother. Against her mother's wishes, she scrambled to follow her friend to safety. The two girls continued to play in the hallway and Lela watched in hopes that the hoodlums would find another place to dwell. They cursed and taunted the old woman for an entire half hour before they grew bored and left. The last of them had just managed to clear the corner when Carla looked for Regina to find her not where she had been instructed to be. So, she dressed quickly and went next door to inquire of her daughter's where-abouts.

There were three doorbells, one for each floor. She rang the first-floor bell. She was not sure of the level on which the girl lived but she started on the ground and would work her way up. Lela answered the door.

"Hello, I'm sorry to bother you but, have you seen my little girl?" Carla had to look down when she spoke because of the elderly woman's handicap.

"Yes, there were some real bad kids teasing the girls and I thought it would be safer if they played in here until the bums were gone. They just left a minute ago. I thought for a minute I might have to call the cops."

Carla understood and was less alarmed. She was just grateful that no harm had come to Regina.

"Won't you come in?" asked Lela. "The girls get along so well and Darla doesn't have any friends. It sure is nice to see that your daughter can look past what my grand-daughter looks like and see how beautiful she is inside. No one else has ever tried to get to know her."

Carla stepped inside to find a dear friend in Lela. Since the escape from Joseph, she had moved to 10th Street and kept completely to herself. She desired to make a better life for herself and her child so, she refrained from the association of the wrong crowd which was prevalent in that rough neighborhood. Though she still drank on occasion she was delusional in believing she would maintain her social drinker status while Lela, on the other hand, indulged daily for courage.

CHAPTER 8

Lela and Carla became extremely close. Carla assisted her with errands that she normally would have to wait for her children to find time to accomplish. She composed a list of groceries and then purchased them along with her own household goods. She then brought the receipt to her grateful friend and was immediately reimbursed. Lela appreciated no longer having to worry about running out of anything before stock could be replenished and in return, Regina was allowed to stay with Darla during the week which made things easier for Carla to pick her up from next door rather than all the way on the other side of the city. Just as the two children spent a great deal of time together, the adults were destined to do the same.

Unfortunately, Carla drank with Lela which caused her to regress back to daily consumption. Soon, that did not carry enough excitement. There was a bar at the intersection of Cumberland and Warnock Streets. To get there required a short walk down 10th and a left. One block down on the right, the pale blue sign which read the words, "The Lucky Tavern" in pink neon script letters, was visible from the corner. Her body longed for the alcohol induced cravings of adrenaline associated with physical altercations and verbal wars. So, Carla spent most Saturdays and Sundays there as she looked forward to the probability of a new episode of drama.

One afternoon, Carla sat at the bar of the tavern sipping Canadian Club on the rocks with a splash. That was her drink of choice. She had no appetite for beer because she disliked the taste. Wine always managed to give her such an intense hangover the next day. So, she sat there in thought while she nursed her beverage, never saying a word to anyone. A man who sat at a booth across from the bar noticed and watched her for about an hour. He had more than enough beer in his system and yet ordered another. The more he ingested, the more intrigued he became with the pretty lady and finally gained enough nerve to go over to strike up a conversation.

"Hey, Good-lookin'," the man spoke in a slurred voice.

"Hello," Carla returned the greeting rather impatiently.

"What's your name, pretty lady?"

"Carla," she replied.

"You want some company?"

"No, I'm just enjoying my drink. I didn't come to meet anybody."

"Oh, what you think you're better than everybody else? You just sittin' over here so high and mighty on your stool!"

"Look Mr., I don't think I'm better than anybody. I just want to sit here and mind my own business. I didn't come here to socialize."

"You can drink alone at home. People come to bars to meet folks."

The bartender knew Carla and listened to the tense conversation. He saw how irritated the stranger made her and found it necessary to interject.

"Hey, Tyrone, leave the lady alone. Didn't you hear her say she just wants to have her drink?"

"Calvin, I ain't talkin' to you! I'm talkin' to the pretty lady here. Why don't you just tend to the bar? You ain't got no business with this lady." Tyrone said in a peevish tone as he drew a barstool closer to Carla's and asked numerous questions. The bartender continued his duties but, still could not help but ease drop.

"Where you live, pretty lady?"

"I live in the neighborhood," she answered and quickly turned her head.

"Can I walk you home?"

"I'm not ready to go home and when I am, I'll be going alone. But, thank you for the offer," she hastily answered.

"You know one damn thing? You sure are a nasty acting bitch."

Carla never responded verbally but she instantaneously threw the drink that she held in his face. The stranger immediately jumped from his stool and began hurling more insults at her. The bartender instructed Carla to go to the rest room and he motioned to the bouncer to throw Tyrone out. When Carla returned, her menace had been silenced and discarded.

"I'm sorry you had to go through that, Carla. I don't know what got into him. He has never bothered anybody before. Well, it's taken care of now, here's another Canadian Club on ice with a splash."

"Thank you."

"You wasted almost a full drink on that old fool so, I thought it would only be fair to replace it on the house," replied Calvin.

"No, I mean thank you for getting rid of my problem," she said as she gave a flirty smile.

"I don't see ladies in here a lot. When I see one, I know to keep an eye on her," boasted the bartender.

"I'm grateful, Calvin." She took several sips from her glass and grabbed her coat.

"Are you gone for the night?"

"Yea, I've had enough. I'm going home."

"Are you gonna be all right or did I need to get one of the guys to walk you home?"

"You put that guy out a while ago. I'm sure as cold as it is outside he's long gone. I'll be fine. But, again thank you!"

Carla stepped out into the winter and found that the temperature had dropped tremendously since she first arrived three hours earlier. She stood in the doorway of the bar while she fastened her coat and placed her gloves that she carried in her purse on her hands for added warmth. She pulled her collar up around her neck and started across the street. She managed to walk half a block on Cumberland and she heard her name.

"Hey Carla!" She kept walking because she recognized the voice as the drunkard from the bar and it was too cold and windy to move slowly. She kept her steps quick.

"I been watchin' you from my friends house across the street. I mean...... I want to walk you home," she heard from a short distance behind her. She immediately picked up the pace.

"Hey, I'm tryin' to be nice to you. I shouldn't be sayin' nothin' to ya' since you threw that drink in my face."

Carla kept walking and obviously the cold had sobered him a bit because he walked with more control and speed than she anticipated. Soon, he was right behind her and she surprised him. She unexpectedly turned around and stopped dead in her tracks to face him eye to eye.

"Why don't you leave me the hell alone? I'm not bothering you. All I wanted was to have a drink and go home in peace. Please, just leave me alone?"

A tall man on his way to the trolley stop heard her shouts at the stalker who called her by name. The gentleman was suddenly compelled to her rescue.

"Hey Carla," he greeted.

Both Tyrone and Carla were surprised to hear her named called and turned in the direction of the voice. "Hey Carla, how are you doing?"

She knew that she had never seen the man in her life but, it was a welcomed interruption so she pretended to know him. "Oh hi. How've you been?" she asked as she looked down at his gloveless, cold hands to view his wedding band.

"I'm doing great. It's good to see you. It's been such a long time, Carla."

"How is your wife doing?" Carla asked with a smile that demanded an extreme effort to make genuine because it was so cold.

"Carla come on," the gentleman said as he handed her his elbow to grasp. It's cold out here. We can talk as we walk."

Carla grabbed the man's arm on cue and they continued the farce as they walked away, arms locked. Tyrone was angry and embarrassed because had been ignored and then left there standing like a fool in the snow. He slowly walked behind them and he crossed the street to give the impression that he was no longer in pursuit. He turned the corner as he noticed Carla's final destination by use of his peripheral vision.

"Thank you so much! What is your name?"

"Walter."

"It was nice of you to walk me home. You didn't have to do it and you went out of your way." She reached into her purse to offer him money.

"You don't owe me anything. I was happy to do it. I'm new to Philadelphia and if my wife found herself in trouble, I would want someone to come to her aid. Keep your money," he insisted.

"Are you sure I can't give you something for your trouble?"

"What I did for you was no trouble at all. It's been a pleasure meeting you," he said as he pointed for her to go inside. He watched her unlock and close the door behind her and he walked and stood at the trolley stop to wait for his ride. From the window of her apartment, she watched Walter rock back and forth to stay warm. It was another twenty minutes before his trolley stopped in front of him and he disappeared forever.

"Chivalry is not dead," she thought to herself. "That was a true gentleman." She continued to stare out the window in disbelief that Walter really had no ulterior motive. He was satisfied just to protect a lady in distress.

CHAPTER 9

Carla returned home from the bar at 4:40 p.m. and decided at 8:00 to go over to Lela's to obtain Regina. She really longed for phone capabilities rather than having to go out in the cold to let her child know that it was time to come home. She wrapped in several layers of clothing and stepped into the snow. Once again she was approached by the man from the bar from behind and she turned to meet a switchblade in her chest.

"There, Miss bitch! I don't see you being uppity now! If you won't be with me, you won't be with nobody!" he said under his breath as he fled away on foot.

"Oh God," Carla moaned as blood soaked her coat within minutes and her glove that tightly clutched the wound became drenched. She stumbled to the front steps of Lela's house and leaned on the door for support as she rang the bell and knocked. Because Darla and Regina were in the back playing, Lela's handicap caused her to take a long while to answer. When the door finally opened, Carla took five steps toward the living room and collapsed onto the floor. Lela acted quickly, not even stopping to ask what happened. She wheeled herself to the front room where the police was called. In the interim, Lela returned to Carla's side in the hallway.

"Carla! Oh Lord! What happened to you?"

"I've been stabbed," she murmured. "...........in my chest."

"It's gonna be all right. You just stay calm! The ambulance is on its way."

Never had Lela felt so helpless as she did at that very moment. She wanted to reach out and stroke Carla's hair for comfort but she could not because her wheel chair obstructed the range of reach. "I'll just keep talking to her," she thought.

"Carla, did you see who did this to you? Did you get a look at his face?"

"He fol.....lowed me from the bar. Calvin, the bar....tender knows him," Carla managed to get out.

"What bar Carla?"

"Lucky Tavern a.....round the co.....rner," she replied just before she passed out.

"Come on Carla, you'd better not die on me. Carla? Carla?"

Lela prayed that her friend was unconscious and not dead. She was so still and the large puddle of blood that developed from the injury grew in size. Lela's disability added to her feeling of total helplessness and knew nothing more to do than to continue to ask God's assistance. The only thing that distracted her from prayer was the sound of the sirens and the flashing lights that penetrated the hallway. She opened the door and pointed where her friend's lifeless body still laid in the pool of blood. The paramedics went straight to Carla and the police hurriedly began their line of questioning. Because the sirens and the commotion could be heard by the entire block, the children pushed past the observing neighbors from the upper levels and came into the hallway. Regina recognized the top of her mother's head and saw the blood.

"Mommy! What's wrong with my mother?" She sounded more and more anxious with every question. "Why is Mommy bleeding?" she asked as she rushed toward the two men in uniform with hand held machines.

Lela yelled to Regina, "Get back in the room. Let these people help your mom!"

Darla pushed Regina back as she struggled to get past. "What's the matter with my mom?" she cried as she continued her efforts to reach her mother but was overcome by Carla's condition.

Lela remembered that she had been given Carla's oldest son's telephone number while she cared for Regina. The instructions were that Carla could not come fast enough on public transportation in the event of an emergency so, William was to be notified. She called Regina into the room from another entrance and handed the phone to her.

"I called your brother William and told him what happened and asked him to come right away," she told her in a calm voice.

"Hello?" the child answered.

"Regina, are you all right?" a masculine voice asked from the other end of the line.

"I'm not hurt, just Mommy. William it's real bad. Are you coming?"

"Yes, I'll be there as soon as I can." He then heard the receiver being handed back to Lela.

William was given the address and Lela asked him to hold the line when she noticed Carla was being placed on a stretcher to be transported to the hospital.

"I'm sorry I had you holding but I needed to hear where they are taking your mother. The ambulance is on its way to Philadelphia General and maybe it would be best if you met Carla there."

"Thank you for calling, I appreciate you being such a good friend," he replied as he apprehensively hung up the receiver.

While Lela finished the conversation with William, Regina returned to the hallway to find her mother being wheeled out of the door.

"Wait for me, I'm going with my Mommy," she yelled to the police. She ran toward them with no coat or hat insisting to be taken to the hospital.

Lela, the woman that Regina affectionately called "Grandma," looked into her eyes and read her pain and anguish. "Sir, her oldest brother is on the way to the hospital to meet the ambulance. He will be responsible for his sister's care and her going with you would save him the trouble of coming back across town to pick her up from here." She appealed to the officer's sensitive side.

"The girl will need her hat and coat." The tall, Caucasian cop with dark hair insisted and Regina returned within a few seconds with her coat half donned and hat in hand. The ambulance doors were being closed just as Regina stepped out onto the snow. Her eyes went directly to the trail of blood which had fallen from her mother's hand while used to cover her wound. She followed in the squad car and was sped through the streets of Philadelphia at a rate in which she had never remembered traveling before. The flashing red lights and sirens promoted pedestrians to scurry out of harm's way.

Regina watched Carla as she was wheeled into the emergency room and tried to speak to her. An officer grasped the child with a tight grip on the shoulder as her mother's stretcher disappeared down a long corridor. The only connection she had to the woman that had given birth to her six years prior was the trail of blood that lined the floor from the entrance door to the double doors at the end of the hall. She paced distressfully back and forth along side the trail. She cried and wondered what was happening and why? One of the officers directed the attention of a young man in a hospital uniform to the trail and he mopped away the drops of blood from the floor. She felt even more anxious now that she no longer had a point of focus.

Regina saw a tall, black man come into the emergency entrance and he talked with the police who had brought her to the hospital. William had met Regina on occasion when she was younger but, Regina was unsuccessful in distinguishing between him and any other stranger in the room. The officers brought him over to the child.

"Your brother William is here now so we have to go back to work." The officers stooped to her level as they spoke. "Everything will be fine. You be a good girl and this will be over before you know it."

"Thank you for helping my mom," she replied with a tearful soft voice.

"We were just doing our job, little girl."

"Well, thank you for doing your job," she replied as she looked into each officer's eyes with sincere gratitude. The tall, blue-eyed officer with blonde hair, stooped down once again and gave Regina a big hug. "You keep being brave for your mom, OK?"

"But, I'm not brave. I'm scared," she replied as more tears streamed down her worried little face.

William realized the officer's need to depart, so he came over to Regina, took her by the shoulders and led her into the nearby waiting area. The officers waved good-bye and Regina returned the gesture as she looked over her right shoulder and walked away. She sat down where there was a TV playing. But, her attentions could not be persuaded in any other direction other than her mother. She looked up at her brother's face and saw concern. He was preoccupied, confused and bewildered as to the events that led up to the current condition of the woman that had also given birth to him.

"Don't worry, everything is going to be all right," she said as she forced a smirk of a smile on her face."

William looked down at his estranged sister and smiled at her seemingly grown up response to his facial expression. He never said a word to her because it was evident she really was no longer in need of comfort. But, he was mistaken. She was merely trying to be brave for the both of them.

CHAPTER 10

Regina and William had taken up temporary residence at the hospital for the past four hours. William was a preacher and had founded his own church (a store front building) some years before. His petition to God on his mother's behalf was all he had to offer for the situation as a doctor appeared in the waiting room.

"Are any of you relatives of Carla Richards?" he asked as he looked around the room.

"I'm William, her son," he said as he stood to meet the surgeon face to face. He looked down in the direction of Regina. "...and this is my sister."

The doctor gave a quick smile as he looked at the child. "William can I talk to you in private for a minute?" The two men walked away from the waiting area and conversed.

"I must be honest with you. It was very touchy there for a moment and we lost her twice during surgery. She is still in very critical condition right now but, we have done all that we can do for her. The rest is up to her. I will let you know though, she definitely has the will to live because when she arrived, she became conscious for a few minutes. All she could say was, "Walk with me Jesus. Please, walk with me?" I don't know what faith she is but I didn't save your mother. Someone higher than me saved her. All we can do now is wait and see what happens."

"Thank God she's alive," William sighed. "All I know is that she was stabbed in the chest but how bad is her injury?"

"Carla was stabbed once in the chest with a switchblade that we guess was approximately four inches long. The knife broke off in her heart and she lost a tremendous amount of blood. We first removed the broken blade and then had to make repairs to the heart itself. We did the very best that we could but it's out of our hands now. Yet, I must tell you that for your mother to be alive right now, she is a very lucky woman!"

"Thank you doctor for all that you've done," William said as he extended his hand for a shake of appreciation.

As their hands connected, "Good luck to you and your family, Mr. Richards," the surgeon responded.

"Thank you, doctor."

William returned to Regina and took a deep breath as he re-entered his seat beside her. "Mom is doing better but she is still real sick. We will just have to wait a while longer."

Two hours later, a nurse came in search of him. "Mr. Richards, your mother wishes to see you." The petite Caucasian nurse escorted William to Carla's bed-side. "She's heavily sedated so you can't visit for very long," the nurse urged.

"William," Carla whispered. "Come closer to me." She then held out her hand for his. "Where is Regina?"

"She's in the waiting room, out front," William informed her.

"Promise me that if anything happens to me, you'll take care of her? Her father could care less about her and his children too. Promise me you'll raise her as your own?"

"You're going to be fine. You're going to be able to raise her yourself. Don't talk like this," William pleaded.

"Just promise me. She has nobody else," she said as her weak eyes met his.

"I'll take care of her for you," he said weakly as though a ferocious punch had taken the wind out of him.

"Son, will you pray with me?"

"Of course I will." He was able to manage a much stronger response.

When his prayer was finished he noticed that Carla had drifted into a deep sleep. William held her hand for a minute more and then left to return to Regina. It was 4:42 a.m. and he found Regina curled up in a single chair. The whole night had been exhausting for him and so much more for her. He woke her and drove to his home in West Philadelphia where she was directed to the sofa and was given a pillow and blanket. There she fell fast asleep until 10:00 a.m. on Sunday morning to find her brother had gone to church several hours earlier. She was in unfamiliar surroundings with total strangers. But, she never behaved as though she was uncomfortable because there was no way to differentiate between strangers or family; they were both.

Regina started school in September of 1968 and was cared for in the evenings by Lela. So, when circumstances forced her to live with her brother indefinitely, she left the friends that she had just become accustomed to and read-justed. Surprisingly, for the first time in her life, she had a sense of normalcy with William. She thought that the upper middle class surroundings of her brother's home classified them as being rich. Little things such as the possession of both a kitchen dinette as well as a separate dining room table with matching chairs, Priscilla curtains verses the bargain store brand and fast food in the freezer of the home were all new experiences for her. The extreme poverty of her household made her brother's abode seem wealthy yet she never viewed her life with her mother as anything other than average.

Carla was hospitalized for approximately four weeks and two days while she recovered from her brutal attack. The police apprehended Tyrone and he was incarcerated for three years. When Carla was well enough to go home, she was taken to William's house and Patsy, who was a housewife, cared for her mother-in-law. It took Carla another four weeks to partially regain her strength. During this entire time, Stouffer's paid their most valuable chef as if she worked every day since her incapacitation and William secured her rent and utilities so that she would have a home to return to when her health mended. Carla's second oldest son, Malvin, interpreted his mother's stay with William as a show of favoritism and voiced those feelings to her when he came occasionally to visit. Because Carla harbored so much guilt for leaving them as young children, the slightest sign of their displeasure prompted irrational behaviors from her.

"Mom, you know what? Bernice can take just as good care of you as Patsy can. Why won't you come and stay with us for a while?"

"Malvin, Willliam is responsible for my bills and rent on 10th Street and it was just easier to come here because he was already keeping Regina for me until I got out of the hospital," she explained.

"I would have taken care of things for you too. But, you chose to ask your favorite son to do everything. You walked away from us. We didn't walk away from you and I love you, Mom. Give me a chance to care for you too." There it was, the infamous guilt trip. He seemed to have packed bags for two people because he stayed on that trip for quite some time.

"Patsy doesn't work and Bernice does. That's a lot of pressure to put on a working woman," she tried to justify.

"I've talked to my wife before I said anything to you and she would
love to have you with us."

"Why move in the condition that I'm still in. It really doesn't make any sense," she replied agitated by his persistence.

William overheard the conversation and feared his mother's recovery would be prolonged by undue stress. "Let Mom get a little stronger and then she can make a decision. Right now I really think she needs to rest, Malvin. Please, can we talk about this later?"

Malvin left, but was unhappy to return home without his mother accompanying him. Carla never gave much thought about the ramifications of the unnecessary move and how it would affect Regina. She had to be removed from school for the second time in one school term and adjust to new classmates as well as Malvin's family. But, all Carla wanted was to appease an adult son who still harbored resentment for her abandonment of him as a child.

William graciously relinquished his mother's responsibilities to his sibling merely because she was insistent. He totally disagreed with her decision, however. Regina was placed in a neighboring school to where Malvin and his wife lived. They also lived in an upper middle class setting but things were not as kosher as the living arrangements with William and Patsy. And yet, Regina adjusted well as usual and her grades never suffered. She always managed to make straight A's even in the midst of family crisis.

CHAPTER 11

C arla found it difficult to live with Malvin and his wife. She always felt as though she was the cause of the blaring arguments she overheard through their bedroom door. She also believed she was the excuse used by Bernice to relinquish her job. Less income in the household caused added tensions between the two of them but, Malvin insisted that his mother was not an imposition nor the source of disagreements between himself and his spouse. Because Carla was an extremely private woman, she really resented Bernice plundering through her personal belongings while she was out of the room for any length of time. The final straw was drawn when Carla realized that her bills were not taken care of as attentively as William had paid them. Therefore, she was forced to speed up her recovery to not allow her own home matters to become too uncontrollable. After three weeks with her second oldest son, she decided to do the rest of her recuperating at home. It was near the end of the first school semester when Carla determined that she should return to her humble abode on 10th Street.

"Mom, I'm tired of moving around. Can I at least finish this school year where I am?" She secretly despised how her life was mishandled and her statement exposed the first sign of Regina's displeasure.

"I'll have to talk with Malvin and Bernice to see if they mind," Carla responded.

"Can you please ask them? It will be just 'til the end of school and I promise not to be any trouble."

Carla made the suggestion and it was agreed that Regina could stay. Bernice took very good care of the child because she always yearned for a girl and had been blessed with two boys. She liked the thought of another female in the house and she treated Regina fairly as if she was her very own daughter. Bernice was on a bowling league and when she went to tournaments, the boys often stayed with their dad.

"Bernice, can I stay here too?" Regina got along well with her nephews and grew close to them quickly.

"Malvin, do you want your sister to stay with you or go with me?" Bernice asked.

"I don't care, it's up to her," he replied hurriedly so as to direct his attentions back to the football game.

Malvin's sons Brent and Cornelius were given pop sickles and chips as a snack. When Regina let it be known that she wished to be given the same, Malvin insisted that there was none left. He played and wrestled with his sons during intermissions and commercials but totally neglected to shower Regina with any affection. After several hours, she felt those old uncomfortable feelings of an outcast resurface. But, Malvin had always treated her with kindness while Carla lived there.

"Malvin, why are you being so mean to me?"

"I'm not being mean."

"You are different from when Mommy was here."

"No I'm not. Just shut up! I'm tryin' to watch the game." Malvin brushed the six year old off like a unwanted crumb from a Thanksgiving Day table.

Regina sat and watched the television screen but her focus was not there. She sat quietly for about an hour without so much as one word. Brent and Cornelius tried to their dismay to distract her back into fun and games but, she was engrossed in feeling ostracized. Finally, she tried to address the subject again in hopes that the old familiar pain of being unwanted would exit as suddenly as it came.

"Malvin, why don't you like me?" she innocently asked.

"What?"

"Why don't you like me? Bernice likes me."

"How do you know Bernice likes you. You're my sister. How could she like you more than I do?"

"I don't know but she does. She must like me because she's always nice to me whether Mommy is around or not. She treats me the same."

"If you don't like it, you can just get out!" He shouted and glared at her for a moment before he looked back in the direction of the game.

The young child's heart sank and tears streamed one after another down her small sad face. She sat there and replayed Malvin's last words over and over in her mind until she became consumed with the urge to just run away. She concluded if she stayed there she would be in no better position than if she walked from 77th and Ogontz Ave. to her home on 10th Street. The distance between the two points was over an hour drive.

Regina was tall for her age but extremely underweight for her height. She stood up and walked over to the heavy oak door which was proven difficult for even an adult to open. She pulled and tugged at the door for twenty minutes with much determination. She finally slid down the door with her knees to her chest and cried. The boys wanted to talk her into staying but their efforts were intercepted by their father.

"Regina what are you doing in the foyer crying," asked Bernice when she returned home.

"Malvin wouldn't give me any pop sickles or chips like he gave the boys. When I asked him why he didn't like me, he told me to get out!" she bluntly explained as she began to sob again.

"Malvin why are you treating your sister that way? You ought to be ashamed of yourself. She is just a child. That was mean to give the boys snacks and give her nothing. How would you feel if somebody treated you that way? I'll tell you. You wouldn't like it at all. I don't know why you did it but you should be very ashamed of treating your baby sister that way."

"Oh Bernice, she's exaggerating. I was just kidding with her. Lord!"

"Well, kidding or not, finding her by the doorway crying means that you hurt her feelings. Come on Regina I'll give you a pop sickle." A torn box with at least four pop sickles could be seen from Regina's height looking up at the open freezer door.

"But, I'm sure he told me there were no more pop sickles." Regina attempted to reassure herself.

CHAPTER 12

"**M**ommy, Malvin locked me in the closet yesterday," Regina explained to her mother who had come to pick her up for the weekend. "He really doesn't like me. Last week, when Bernice went bowling, he told me to get out."

"Bernice do you know what she's talking about?" Carla inquired of his wife because he was at work.

"Yes, Mom. Malvin said that he was just playing with her," Bernice replied.

"Did he tell her that he was just playing?" Carla really was not ready to challenge Malvin's motives because she refused to think anything but good about him. Guilt had her paralyzed.

"No."

"Regina, he was just playing with you. You know how Malvin is," Carla stated. "We will talk about this when we get home." Carla saw the frustrated look on the child's face.

"I don't want to talk about this anymore. I just want to go home with you and stay," Regina said.

"You were the one who didn't want to switch schools again. Now, you're telling me that you have changed your mind?" Carla asked the question in order to truly get a feel for what the youngster wanted.

"Yes, I just want to be with you, Mommy."

Arrangements were made and Regina returned to her old school. She miraculously readjusted to her surrounding once more and still her grades never suffered. However, she learned more from her home life than she was able to forget. She learned how to avoid troubling confrontations by not talking about them and to deal with the offender as less as possible. She learned not to resolve an issue but to escape it. But, those situations as traumatic as they were, had not been forgotten. The ill relationship between herself and the Ulzler children, the lack of her father's attention, the molestation, her mother's attack or Malvin's mistreatment of her could not actually be disregarded because they were all left unresolved. She wondered what she was sure of because of the constant denial of others involved. She no longer had a concept of truth because she had been called a liar and exaggerator when she told what she knew to be the truth. Their excuses for what was done always minimized her feelings. They made her seem as though she had done something wrong. So, the memories were tucked away only to resurface as future traumatic events unfolded in her life. She too had been molded to become a part of the family's curse of secrets and those secrets were nightmares that she could not be awakened from.

Carla went back to Stouffer's a few weeks before she was completely recovered but managed to regain her strength in spite of her premature return. She paced herself and prepared before and after work for the following day so that she could keep up. One evening as she prepared apple fitters, a familiar face came through the door to embark upon a meal. It was Frank Barker whom she met months earlier and had been kind enough to give her a ride home during the first snow storm of the year. She recognized him immediately and found herself quite pleased to see him. She had no way of contacting him nor would she have done so but; she hoped that he was intrigued enough to make an effort to speak again.

He mouthed to her across the restaurant. "What time do you get off?" He wanted to time his meal accordingly.

"So, you've finally finished for the evening?" Barker asked as she presented herself at his table side.

"Yes, it's very nice to see you again. I wasn't sure that I would." Carla remembered how abruptly she had gotten out of his car the night that he transported her home from work.

"I've spent every day since then thinking about you but my job takes me out of town quite a bit."

"What do you do?" Carla was curious to know.

She showed the first real interest in Barker and he took notice. He viewed their first meeting as mere flirting. "I work for Amtrak as a Pullman porter. Sometimes I'm gone for weeks at a time. And the last thing I want to talk about while I am at home is work. Can I give you a ride home?"

Carla was delighted that he asked. "Yes, I really would appreciate it." Since the stabbing, she found walking made her easily out of breath. "Then on the way, I can fill you in on what's been going on in my life." She explained about her attack and how she lived with two sons to recuperate. Then, their conversation turned to where their last one had ended.

"You see, that's what I mean. If you had a phone, you wouldn't have had to go out to get your daughter. You could have called for her. I know I was a stranger to you when I offered but, I want you to have one. Please let me do it? I have my own selfish reason for wanting it anyway. I don't want to have to come to eat just to see you or hear your voice. Will you let me put it in?"

"The last thing I need is another bill to pay. I don't make that much money and I have a child to raise," Carla argued.

"Your safety is needed for raising your daughter wouldn't you think? I'll put the phone in your name but, I'll pay the deposit and bills if I have to."

Carla had nothing to say in response because she knew that he was right. But, she was not well acquainted with this man and yet he was offering her something. She could not help but to wonder what plot he had planned.

"What is he up to?" She thought to herself. "Maybe he just wants to be nice."

Her mind flashed back to the gentleman who pretended to know her which saved her from Tyrone on the street the day of her attack. "He didn't want anything. He was just happy to be able to help me. That does prove that every man is not just after what he can get," she convinced herself. She had spent the remainder of the ride home thinking about Barker's offer and she looked up to find that she had reached her destination.

"Can we sit here and talk for a while before you go in?" Barker obviously wanted more of Carla's time. He parked the blue Cadillac and kept the engine running. They talked for over an hour and Carla decided that it would be safe to invite him in.

"It doesn't make sense to have you burn all your gas while we talk. Would you like to come in for a while?"

"I have a long day but, I will come in for a few minutes." He was pleased for the invitation.

"Do you drink? All I drink is Canadian Club and you are welcome to it if you'd like?"

Barker drank occasionally and did not want to turn down any offer Carla extended to him, so he graciously accepted. " Make mine on the rocks."

Carla poured the drinks and they sat at the dinette table conversing for another two hours. Since her hospitalization and medications for recovery, that was her first drink in over three months. The whiskey affected her quickly Barker noticed and he found it necessary to excuse himself.

"I'll come by tomorrow to make arrangements for the phone," he said as he kissed her on the cheek and said good-bye.

Barker honored his word of the day before and picked Carla up to handle business. He also realized how much this woman had begun to mean to him in such a short time. He was no longer trying to win her affections for proof to himself. He actually and genuinely cared for her which came as quite the surprise to him. Unfortunately, the relationship would grow rapidly to go nowhere because Carla's general nature since Geoffrey was to insist on the attention that she favored. Barker's position with the railroad did not give room for their interest to blossom.

CHAPTER 13

Carla was on her way to work one evening and crossed paths with an older man, Jay Wilson, who was ten years her senior. He was tall, dark skinned with large dark brown eyes. He was an immaculate dresser and carried himself to be exceptionally educated. He was attractive even though his features were not commonly referred to as handsome. That day, he was one stop away from his destination and was drawn in by Carla's beauty as she entered the trolley. Instead of getting off at his stop, he decided to continue his ride to give himself the advantage of master minding a conversation with her. She had not noticed him right away. She was standing near Jay holding on to a pole to steady herself as the trolley car swayed back and forth over the cobblestone street. He tugged at the gentleman's coat directly beside Carla to recruit his efforts with the hope of gaining the woman's attention. When she realized that Jay was motioning to her to relinquish his seat, she smiled and moved in his direction. Then he strategically stood himself in front of her.

"He is wearing the whitest starched shirt I have ever seen," Carla thought as she inspected him from head to toe.

His suit was freshly dry-cleaned and his shoes were polished and buffed to a high shine like those of a military man. She could not possibly fail to notice his beautiful, straight, gleaming white teeth and his lint free, felt fedora which fit his head as if it was tailored just for him. The camel wool coat which covered the suit complimented his broad shoulders and reminded her of the perfect fit of clothes on mannequins of the up-scale department stores where she could only afford to window shop. His nails were clean and well trimmed and he wore no jewelry except for the expensive watch that adorned his left wrist. He clutched a rolled newspaper under his left arm and held on to the pole with his right hand.

"He must have a very important job. He obviously knows how to make the best of what he has been given as far as his appearance," assessed Carla.

She was interrupted by his calm, strong, authoritative voice. "Where are you headed this evening, Miss?" Carla made it a habit of dressing at work and therefore her attire did not give any clue to where she was going.

"I'm going to work. I work the night shift." She smiled as she gave her answer.

"You must hear this all the time but, you are one beautiful woman," Jay complimented.

Soon after his comment, the seat beside Carla became available but Jay looked around to see if there were any other women standing. He was such a gentleman, articulate and charming as well. He gestured to an older woman standing behind him that he was saving the seat for her. Carla was now impressed.

"Where are you headed, Sir?" Carla was both sarcastic and interested at the same time and Jay immediately recognized it.

"Well, I was headed home about ten stops ago before you came and turned my head."

" Do you mean to tell me that you have been riding ten stops past yours just to talk to me?" she asked in that same sarcastic tone. "Where are you going now that I have turned your head?"

"Where ever you highness is going," he flirted as he flashed his pearly whites.

What a dashing smile it was and it made Carla warm all over. He was witty and had a wonderful sense of humor. She loved his outgoing personality. It was very appealing without being overbearing and that sparked a curiosity about him that could not be quenched on one trolley ride. He feared that she would be reaching her stop soon.

"I would love to finish this conversation but we are coming to the end of the line. How can I talk with you again?" he asked.

"Meet me at the stop where I got on, tomorrow at the same time and you'll have your chance to finish our conversation," Carla smiled.

"I will do just that! What do I call you? I don't even know your name!" he shouted as she rushed to catch her next trolley.

She was gone but, he knew that he would wait at the stop for her the next day so all was not lost. The next day arrived slowly for him but, Jay anxiously watched at the corner of 10th and Cumberland to see the beautiful young lady he had met the day before. He was disappointed to find that she was not there. His anxiety continued daily until on the third day, there she stood. She entered and positioned herself behind the driver because there were no vacant seats. She looked around to view Jay coming towards her from the back.

"I don't know why I keep giving up my seat just to be near a woman that has stood me up for the last two days," Jay said wearing a scowl on his face.

Carla saw right through the façade. "I forgot to tell you that I'm off on weekends. I just wanted to see if you really rode the same trolley every day or if you were just telling me what I wanted to hear."

"Oh, so it was a test?" If it had been, he knew he passed.

"No, how can truth be a test?"

He found her as witty as well as beautiful and that was an attractive combination for him. Again, he rode the trolley to the end of the line and said his fair well. He immediately wondered how long the rides out of his way would continue before he could really get to know the woman who had his interest but had not chosen to identify herself. On the sixth ride to the end of the line, the inquiry was found to be complete.

"If my stop is the one after you get on, that must mean that you live near here?" He made the statement sound more like a question. He was definitely fishing for more information. She had let the bait dangle for days just to see how committed he was to find out more about her and he was more than committed.

"Look Jay, today is Friday and I'm off for the weekend. You've ridden past your stop every day this week and one day last week. What do you hope to gain by doing this every day?" she asked.

"It's not what I hope to gain, it's what I've gained already. I enjoy just looking at you and I look forward to our talks even if it is on a noisy trolley filled with people. I'd rather talk with you under these conditions than talk to the average woman in the privacy of her own home. I'll take whatever I can get. Not knowing your name will not change the fascination that I have with you nor will it cease the intrigue that has increased each time I've spoken with you. I will ride this trolley indefinitely just to be with you."

That answer was more than she had hoped for. "My name is Carla and I enjoy your sense of humor. I haven't had a lot of happiness in my life and each day, I look forward to meeting you on the trolley because I've come to expect the laughter. Yes, I do love the way you make me smile. Do you have a pen? I'll give you my telephone number."

There was joy over the knowledge of gaining her telephone number at long last. But, there was a sadness in his eyes that she could not quite explain.

"No. I don't have a pen," he replied.

She reached into her purse and took out a eyebrow pencil and scratched her number onto a napkin she had used to wipe off excess lipstick. "Here, call me tomorrow after 4:00 and we may be able to talk more."

He took the napkin and placed it into his pocket. She could see that he was pleased to have it but the sadness that suddenly appeared never left him. It remained on her mind and she could not shake the effects of his expression even when they parted.

CHAPTER 14

The fact that Carla could furnish a contact number to anyone was due to Fred Barker. He called periodically to see how life was progressing for her and those calls caused guilt over the fact that she felt inclined to share her telephone number with Jay. Even though Barker was not her boyfriend or lover, she still felt the telephone obligated her to think twice about allowing anyone else in her life. She did not welcome the conviction and decided to reimburse the deposit to him and pay for the bill herself when it arrived. Barker was not accessible enough for her and Jay's availability made him much more appealing.

"Hello, Carla. This is Jay. How are you doing?"

"I'm fine. I see you called me at 4:00 on the dot. Are you always on time?" Carla liked punctuality in a man.

"Yes, I try to be. Actually I was really looking forward to talking to you again so I watched the clock."

Carla laughed. "Are you always such a smooth talker?"

"I'm not a smooth talker, I just tell you what I feel. There is just no beating around the bush, that's all." He knew his articulation was quite the advantage.

"There's a lot of noise in the background. I can barely hear you at times." Carla informed Jay so that he could either relocate himself or speak into the receiver in a louder voice.

"I'm at my sister's house and she's got a lot of people visiting. There really isn't any better way to talk with you other than in person." He had no desire to converse by telephone and he voiced his preference to speak to Carla face to face.

"Do you want to just call me back later?" Carla used the question to gain knowledge of his evening itinerary.

"No, what I want is to take you to dinner or for a drink. Can I do that? Or can I come and get you and bring you to meet my sister, Katherine? There is plenty of food and drink here. But, it's whatever you would prefer."

"You want me to meet your sister already? I should be getting scared. Next you'll be asking to marry me." Carla was being sarcastic again.

"Wouldn't you like to know? But, right now I just want you to meet my sister, that's all."

Carla gave Jay her address and she was given a estimation of his arrival time.

"I want you to turn every head here, so wear bells," he encouraged.

Katherine and Carla connected from the very beginning. Soon after her arrival, Carla was introduced to all the guests as Jay's girlfriend. Every room of the house was filled with people who were laughing, drinking and talking loudly. It was Katherine's 47th birthday and her family and friends were more than willing to aid in her celebration. Carla was offered a drink and she accepted merely to be sociable. Canadian Club had not been bought for this function so she tried vodka and orange juice. She hated the taste when she took a small sip and decided to hold onto the glass just as a prop.

Jay tried his best to get back to her side but was grabbed by friends and relatives who obviously had not seen him in a very long time. Each person would say, "Long time no see, Jay. Where've you been hiding?"

Carla and Jay's eyes met from across the room and each one found it impossible not to smile back at the other. It took over an hour for the two to be reunited.

"I see you are still nursing that drink Katherine made for you when you first got here. What's the matter, don't you drink?" Jay had noticed because he had not been able to take his eyes off Carla the entire night.

"Yes, I drink a little but, I only drink Canadian Club. There is none here and I wanted to be friendly," Carla responded with a smile.

"Oh hell, we can do something about that. Hey, Bobby! My lady only drinks Canadian Club and we don't have any. Go over to the liquor store and get two fifths for me. Here's the money and keep the change." Jay handed his cousin a twenty dollar bill.

"I'm not the only one not drinking. I haven't seen you drink anything tonight," Carla added.

"I'll get around to it. I just want you to enjoy yourself," he said.

The southern belle/city girl loved all of the attention Jay and his family showered upon her and was made to feel like a celebrity in the house full of strangers in no time at all. But, alcohol consumption was extreme that night and small disagreements escalated into fist fights in minutes. Jay was unaccomplished in obtaining his drink or the two fifths of Canadian Club because he found it more necessary to ascertain their coats and flee the scene before the police arrived.

"I'm sorry for the forced exit, Carla. I don't know why they were acting so foolish."

Carla laughed as she replied, "Did you see the way your uncle fell up against the wall when that large woman shoved him backwards? It was like something from the movies."

"Yeah, it was rather funny wasn't it?" Jay added with a chuckle.

They walked arm and arm as they laughed and talked on their way to the trolley stop. The more they walked, the closer they were drawn to each other. Jay's description of the events of that night seemed so much funnier through his eyes and Carla found herself doubled over at times with the humor that he added to an already comical evening. They arrived back at her house.

"Is it all right if I come by to see you tomorrow?"

"Yes, I'd like that, Jay."

"I'll come by at 1:00, OK?"

"I'll see you then." Carla watched over her shoulder as she unlocked the front door of her building.

Jay excused himself for the evening and whistled all the way to the trolley stop. He was not accustomed to the type of woman Carla was and yet he knew that his comfort with her was as it had never been with anyone.

CHAPTER 15

Regina's father, Joseph, was given the telephone number so that when he wished to visit her, arrangements could be made. One of his many excuses to not see his daughter was that he had no way of contacting her. Now, Regina was seven and found herself envying her brother's children, her nieces and nephews, who had their father's affection. And she coveted that for herself. It was true that she did not desire a closeness with the Ulzler siblings because of their treatment of her. But, she never once stopped dreaming of a relationship with her father.

On June 22, 1970; Regina insisted that she be taken to visit her father for his birthday. Even though she had minimal contact or conversations with him since their separation from his provision, she possessed the strongest unexplained urge to spend time with him on his special day. Carla did not resist. She never tried to encourage or force Joseph to visit with Regina but if the child mentioned the need, the wish was automatically granted. They walked the long ten blocks to Sergeant Street and found that the house and its contents had barely weathered the storm of use. Not much had changed in the five years since their departure.

All the children were gone. The second set of ten followed a mirror image of the lives of their older siblings. Either they had evolved enough to be on their own or became run-aways. They had not all been seen together since the death of their grandfather (Elvena's husband). Everything was the same and yet everything was very different from the way that Regina remembered. When they entered, the smell of both stale and fresh smoke filled the air. But, Regina's focus was not on the building, she was overjoyed just to lay eyes on her father and the smile on her face informed Carla of how well worth the walk to see him had been.

"Hi, Daddy," said Regina.

"Hi there," Joseph responded.

"She just had to see you on your birthday," Carla interjected.

"That's nice. That's real nice." Joseph struggled for conversation because of major guilt and lack of genuine interest.

So, there they sat in strange silence for a few minutes before Carla suggested that Regina give Joseph the birthday card purchased with money that had been given as a gift to her.

"Here Daddy," she said as she handed the envelope bearing his name written by Regina on front. She exhibited such pride while he read it. He finished, then he looked inside the envelope as though he was sure that he had missed something. He reopened the card and once again peered inside in disbelief.

"What's the matter, Daddy?" Regina noticed the disturbed expression on his face.

"Where's the money?" he asked.

"What money, Joseph?" Carla frowned as she looked into his eyes.

"The money that came with the card. She couldn't have just gotten me a card. What good is a card except to put money in it for somebody's birthday."

"Hell, she gave you the card out of the kindness of her heart. You should be grateful. With all of the time and attention you don't spend with her; it's a wonder that she even wants to see you at all. You've got some nerve! You will never change. You won't change one bit! All you ever can think about is what somebody can do for you. I don't ask your ass for a dime to support her even though people say that I'm crazy for letting you off so easy. If anything, you should be giving her money not her giving money to you. Shit! You're the damn father not her. You are one sorry piece of a man, Joseph Ulzler! I hope to God that you rot in hell for being the mean and hateful bastard you are!" Carla was furious and could not control the anger that she had allowed to fester for the past five years.

Regina sat there in disbelief initially and then her emotions received the better of her. "I will not cry," she told herself as she listened to her parents argue. But, it was inevitable. The tears fell. And soon after, she was sobbing uncontrollably.

"I'll never reach out to him again. It hurts too bad to keep trying to love him and he doesn't love me. This will be the last time ever," she promised.

Carla grabbed her purse and her daughter's hand and stormed out of the house. She did not even glance back as he yelled obscenities at them both. On the walk home, nothing was said. Carla did not consider how deeply the child had been impacted. But, she knew from previous situations that Regina was strong enough to adjust to yet another bad situation. That had to have been her limit though, because she never adjusted. She just camouflaged the pain with her good attitude and positive disposition.

Carla and Jay had become very close and she shared with him what had transpired for them that day. Because he himself was childless and as kind as he was, he automatically sympathized and determined within himself that he would give Regina the fatherly love she so desperately sought. Jay made major efforts for each holiday that meant so much to a child. He overcompensated with gifts for Christmas, her birthday; and for Easter, he bought an entire outfit for the morning and a separate one for the evening. His motives were pure and Regina learned quickly to appreciate what she was offered by Jay verses what had been neglected by her own father. He treated the child with such love and adoration. He made her feel special.

Carla prepared dinner in the kitchen that evening when the phone rang. She was able to afford only one telephone and it was located in the bedroom/living room where Jay and Regina were preoccupied with toys.

"Jay, my hands have flour all over them. Can you get the phone?" Carla yelled from her location in front of the stove.

"Hello?" Jay answered.

"I dialed the wrong number," the male voice on the other end responded.

A few seconds later, the telephone rang again and Jay answered. The caller did not bother to speak but cancelled the call. This infuriated Jay and he stood beside Carla in the kitchen and grumbled for a few minutes. Forty-five minutes after the last hang up, there was a knock at the door of the bedroom entrance. Jay answered to find Barker on the other side and each man was just as shocked to see the other.

"Is Carla here?" Barker asked without remotely trying to be polite.

"And who the hell are you?" Jay snarled as he glared at the stranger eye to eye.

Carla heard Barker's voice from the kitchen and quickly presented herself between the two. "Oh, hello Barker. What are you doing here?"

"I came to see you but I see you're busy," as he directed his stare in Jay's direction.

"Hell yeah, she's busy so why don't you carry your ass away from here." Jay did not appreciate the arrogant demeanor of the sharply dressed visitor who was very stiff competition.

Carla intervened. "Why didn't you call before you came over?"

"I did but this jack-ass kept answering the phone," he explained.

Jay lunged toward Barker. "Who the hell are you calling a jack-ass? I'll whip your little smug, plump ass!"

"Barker, I think you had better leave," Carla pleaded.

"Why do I have to leave? Why don't you make him leave?"

"Fred Barker, I'm asking you to leave my house. Please, go!" Carla insisted.

CHAPTER 16

C arla and Jay spent more time together as each day passed. She shared with him her childhood through to her last relationship with Regina's father. After quite some time had passed, she finally shared the gruesome knife attack. But, she was surprised by Jay's experiences which were very unanticipated. She learned that he was born in a small town in Alabama and yet he spoke with no southern accent. He grew up with six other brothers and sisters where they shared the same room as well as the same bed. As articulate and educated as he presented himself, his only form of education was in the world of hard knocks because he had never gone to school a single day of his life. He ran away at the age of five and used the railroad freight cars to move from state to state. It took his ability to think quickly and his wit to avoid police, authorities and foster care and he was quite the master of such, even at that early age.

He listened intently when people spoke and conversations with the men and women on the freight cars who had been abandoned by lady luck proved to be the most beneficial. The majority of drifters were well spoken, educated and intelligent but had somehow fallen upon misfortune for one reason or another. Some had been around the world and he loved the stories of other lands and languages. He maximized every opportunity that presented itself his way. He was well traveled and his only dislike was not being able to bathe more frequently because he detested being dirty. He vowed that when he was old enough to hold a job, no matter what the salary; he would not allow himself to be judged by others according to his appearance or his lack of education. He would be the exception for every stereotypical pattern that set itself up against him. He was proof that you could not judge a book by its cover.

Jay possessed the exceptional quality of being able to persuade a stop sign to walk. He talked his way into jobs and just verbalized his desire to place proof into action. He had never had to fill out an application because his self-confidence, courage and common sense proved to be his most valuable asset.

Carla found herself in awe. Not for his natural talents but for his brightness and intelligence in spite of the lack of education which was not obvious at all.

She recognized the sad look in his eyes the day she gave him her telephone number and name. It derived from his inability to read or write. Her number had been dialed by his sister, Katherine, when he telephoned her and he realized with every available moment he spent with Carla, it would soon become mandatory to reveal his inability. Carla was charmed, romanced and impressed by the man; not by money, car or possessions. Yet, surprisingly, all still was not yet discovered that day.

It was Christmas again and Stouffer's planned an elegant and festive party for all employees. Carla asked Jay to accompany her there. When they walked into the restaurant that evening, all eyes were glued because Carla was absolutely stunning with her natural beauty accentuated by cosmetics. In the two years she worked for the cuisine giant, she was the only black and was never seen by her coworkers outside of her chef uniform or in make-up. She wore an evening dress which was silver sequined from shoulder to the bust-line and the remainder was black velvet. The lights of the restaurant reflected little beads of light onto her face. She was simply enchanting. Jay was impeccably dressed and as usual, he complimented her well. Jay socialized and was the life of the party and she was in amazement that no setting was found to be a discomfort zone for him.

" I enjoyed myself tonight. Thank you for coming with me." Carla smiled as she looked out onto the snow covered street from her window.

"So did I. So much so until I don't want it to stop. I love you and have loved you since the first day I met you. Because I love you, I also love your daughter as if she was my own. I want to take care of you and cherish you daily during the good and the bad times in your life. I want to be your protector and lover and friend. I know that I don't have much to offer you, but I will give you all that I have. I'll make you happy if you do me the honor of becoming my wife."

She was totally astonished but very willing to take him up on his offer. "Yes, I'll marry you."

They were married on January 12th in a little courtroom by the Justice of the Peace. They celebrated that evening at his sister's house. Katherine served as one of the witnesses and was so proud of her brother and the mate he had chosen for himself because she felt that he had finally found a woman who could appreciate him for his special qualities and the man that he fought to become. Up until then, Carla had never witnessed Jay drink. He was happy. He was celebrating his marriage to her as he drank six beers and became so intoxicated until her assistance was needed for his safe arrival home. She laid him across the bed fully dressed and watched him sleep.

CHAPTER 17

Jay insisted Carla quit her job at Stouffer's so he could be the sole provider of her needs. All she was responsible for was household duties because Jay loved her cooking and enjoyed their family life together. Little Regina shared with her new father what she learned in school and each time she did, Jay acquired new knowledge. If he heard it once it became a permanent part of him.

Unfortunately, he and his wife started endulging together daily and with each passing day, Jay consumed more and more alcohol. When the weekend arrived, they would go on binges with the end result being both in a drunken stupor. One Friday night, Carla and Jay argued in the midst of drinking and the situation got totally out of control. Jay had been drinking beer as usual and he then joined Carla with whiskey which he had never done before. It was as if the liquor drove him temporarily mad.

Carla had a reputation for being able to say piercing and hurtful things in the heat of anger but nothing could justify the provocation of Jay's behavior as he slapped her face and she immediately screamed to Regina to go into the kitchen away from the commotion. She then retaliated and their first physical fight took place. It is not known what the altercation was derived from but it was brutal. Regina could hear crashes and objects fall, curses, screams and the shifting of furniture.

Jay's mind flashed back to some of the days on the railroad where he had to battle for his life. He no longer envisioned Carla as his wife, he saw her as a threat to his very survival. There was a straight, iron piece of plumbing pipe that Jay wrapped and taped with newspaper. He did not own a weapon and because he lived in the 10th Street apartment, he needed some sort of protection when he walked to and from the trolley stop. Jay strolled with the iron pipe as it visibly swung in his hand to deter thugs whom possibly possessed an assault plan which involved him as their victim. The newspaper gave more secured control and he reached in the corner, snugly gripped the pipe and beat Carla with it. Regina heard the cursing stop and the small apartment rang with the sound of her mother as she screamed Jay's name.

"Jay, don't!" Carla yelled to him as she threw up her arms to protect her head and face from the blows. Jay repeatedly struck her until she was unconscious and bloody from head to foot. The physical exertion sobered him more quickly than was normal and fear seized him when his eyes viewed the consequences of his intoxication. Carla's lifeless body had fallen to the floor. Her face was covered in blood from the open wounds in her head, on her cheek and top lip. Both arms and legs were bleeding from the blows they sustained also. Her prince charming, had a dark side and now he was afraid that he had killed his princess.

"Oh God, it's so quiet in there. It's too quiet. But, I can't go out there. My mom told me to stay in the kitchen and not to come out for anything."

The silence and the absence of voices made Regina extremely nervous. Several minutes went by and the only sound was Jay's shoes as he paced back and forth. He did not know what to do.

"Lord, what have I done. I shouldn't have mixed that beer and whiskey together."

He rushed over to Carla and felt for a pulse and he found it even though it was very faint. He undressed her down to her bare body and struggled to get her over to the bed. Blood was everywhere. He grabbed a wash cloth and towel from the chest then opened the apartment door and rushed down the hall to the bathroom. He wet the cloth and towel and rushed back to clean the blood from his wife's face. But, too much was coming too fast and within seconds, the wash cloth and the towel were soaked. He decided to pick her up and transport her to the bathroom. He covered her naked body with a bed sheet; dead weight made her seem heavier. Even though she was not larger than a size 14, Jay found it difficult to lift her from the bed.

Regina could not bear the suspense any longer. As long as she could hear movement in the next room she was better able to obey her mother's command to stay in the kitchen. But, now there was that awful silence again. She peeped her small frightened face into the bedroom/living room to find blood everywhere. This sight propelled her to boldness and she looked over toward the entrance that was left standing wide open. She tip-toed out of the apartment and walked slowly and close to the wall to where the blood trail on the floor led. She arrived directly in front of the bathroom door as Jay placed Carla's naked, blood drenched body into the old fashioned freestanding tub filled to its capacity with water. He lowered her in and instantaneously, it changed from clear to dark red and the weight of her body caused the mixture to overflow onto the linoleum floor. Carla's head slid under water and Jay scrambled to pull it above.

"Mommy!" Regina yelled and Jay jerked his neck in the direction of the small voice.

She was scared by the glazed look in his eyes and the unknown condition of her mother. She turned quickly and raced down the stairs, out the front door and headed straight for Germantown Avenue where she knew there was always a strong police presence. She ran as fast as her little legs would carry her and when she arrived at her destination, she spotted an officer's car. The policeman saw that she was in distress and needed urgent help by the fact that she was without a coat in the dead of winter with snow on the ground, she was breathing heavily, sweating and she was flushed from running.

"Please officer, my mother is dead.....I think, Ah. ....She's bleeding bad. Please, help me?" she managed to get out in between breaths.

"OK, slow down. Take it easy."

"No, she could be dead you've ....got to come now!" She was frantic."

The officer radioed for back up and another policeman came out of the store and hurried to get in the car. Regina was placed in the back of the squad car as she gave her address. She was in a police car again for the second time in two years being rushed to her mother's aid. Regina explained what caused her to scurry out of her home in such a hurry and the information was given to head-quarters by radio. When the car pulled up to the house, Regina sprung out and rushed up the stairs. Both officers kept pace with the child and they noticed the smeared blood which led to the closed bathroom door. The apartment door was closed as well and the officer knocked hard.

"Open up, it's the police!" they informed.

Jay opened the door quickly and pointed to Carla whom he had placed back on the bed.

"She needs help!"

One officer's eyes investigated the room thoroughly while the other checked to see if the ambulance was any closer to location.

"What's your name, Sir?" an officer directed his question to Jay.

"Jay Wilson."

"Can you tell me what happened here?"

"My wife fell down the steps and now she's unconscious."

"Why is she naked and wrapped in a bed sheet if she fell down the steps?"

"There was so much blood, I just tried to clean her up but she was too heavy for me." There was that quick wit Carla ironically found so appealing.

The interrogating officer looked in the direction of his partner who tried to get a response from the injured woman. He gave a non-verbal message that he did not believe what had just been stated. The lights from the ambulance could faintly be seen on the second floor but, Regina ran down to show the paramedics where they were needed.

"My God! What happened to this woman?" the paramedic asked the officers.

"Her husband says that she fell down the stairs," the officer answered in a tone of disbelief. Then he turned his attention to Jay.

"Why didn't you call an ambulance for your wife when you saw she was hurt from her fall down the steps?" he asked as he looked over to see the phone by the bed with specks of blood on it. The responding officer continued the informal interrogation.

"I can't read or write, officer," embarrassed by what he had to admit to perfect strangers.

Carla was rushed to Philadelphia General. The officers looked over the rest of the apartment and the hallway. One officer noticed the bathroom door was locked and yelled to Jay to open it. He handed the key to the second officer, who in return took it to his partner. Regina was left alone with Jay.

"What did you tell the police happened to your mother?" Jay asked Regina.

"I didn't tell them anything. I just told them that my mom was bleeding and I wasn't sure if she was still alive..... and for them to please come and help her," Regina explained.

"Well, if anyone asks you what happened to her you'd better tell them that she fell down the steps, OK?"

Regina never responded but just looked at Jay as if she had never spent a tender moment with him in her life. His behavior was not of the man she had grown to love.

"Did you hear me? You tell everybody that she fell ...." He looked at her with much fear and saw the officers coming into the room out of the corner of his eye. He loosened the grip that he originally held on Regina's shoulders and made it appear as though his hands served as a show of support.

"Is this your father?" The officer pointed to Jay.

"He's my stepfather," Regina replied with a voice that was full of emotion.

"Can you tell us what happened to your mom?"

Regina was scared half out of her wits and confused. She was totally ignorant as to what really happened and she definitely did not want Jay to dislike her. Before she could say anything, she burst hysterically into tears. Nothing she said to the police officers made any sense as she babbled.

"Mr. Wilson, have you been drinking?"

"Yes, I had a beer and some whiskey." Jay gave a partially honest answer.

"We noticed the liquor bottle and I can smell alcohol on your breath. But, we also know that you want to get to the hospital to check on your wife so we won't detain you."

"Yes, I have to take the trolley so I need to be on my way. I'm going to see if the next door neighbor can watch Regina while I go. He retrieved the phone receiver and then dialed Lela.

Both officers looked at each other and waited for him to return the phone to its cradle. "We thought you couldn't read or write?"

"I can't but, my wife helped me memorize important numbers and taught me how to dial them."

"And your wife didn't teach you how to call the police or an ambulance?"

"No, not yet," Jay admitted. Jay's calm demeanor served as room for much suspicion. He was too settled for a man whose wife was in such terrible physical condition.

"Don't leave town or anything. We definitely have more questions for you."

"I won't. And thank you both for coming. I really appreciate your help." Jay made eye contact with both officers.

They left but Jay was scared. He did not know whether Carla would live or die and he did not want to go to prison for assault or murder. He continued where he left off before the police returned from the bathroom.

"If you tell anyone that I did this, I swear I'll kill you. If anybody asks you, she fell down the steps!"

He took Regina over to Lela's and no one was sure whether he was in route to see his wife or not.

CHAPTER 18

Regina was left with Lela two days without one word from Jay regarding Carla or his stepdaughter. All that was known was what little information Jay had given his neighbor when he asked for her assistance. Regina was extremely stressed about her mother's condition and inquired of Lela at least once an hour which only prompted frustration on both parts.

"Maybe Jay had called Carla's son, William, and he could shed some light on the situation or at least find information," Lela thought.

"Hello, may I speak to William, please?" Lela hoped William would answer.

"He's not in right now. Can I take a message?" his wife asked.

"Yes this is, Lela Whitfield, his mother's neighbor. Could you tell him to call me as soon as he gets in?"

"Is something wrong, Ms. Whitfield?" Patsy was concerned.

"Well, I'm not sure. I have not heard from Jay since he dropped Regina off over here night before last and the child keeps asking how her mother is doing. Has William heard anything from the hospital?" Lela's voice reflected her bewilderment.

"Hospital? What's wrong with Mom, Carla?" Now Patsy was alarmed.

"I'm not sure but Jay said something about her falling down the steps. I asked Regina but I couldn't get any straight answers from her. I saw the police and ambulance over there but I thought it was for one of the other apartments in that building since I had not heard anything from Carla."

"I'll get in touch with William. He's at the church and I will have him call you. What's your number?"

Lela was now out of her mind with worry because it was obvious her friend's family had no knowledge of the where or why of Carla's disappearance. So, she remained by the phone anxiously waiting for William's return call. Within twenty minutes her phone rang.

"Hello," she answered only having let it ring once.

"Hello, Ms. Lela, this is William. My wife told me you have Regina and you don't know where my mother is. Have you heard from Jay?"

"No, that's why I called you to see if you knew anything," Lela replied.

" So, where is my mother?"

"I don't know. All I can manage to get out of Regina is that she was taken to the hospital." It was apparent that William had even less information than she did.

"I'll be right over to pick up my sister but, I'll try to find out something first." William hung up the phone.

His mother's chaotic lifestyle was causing him much more grief than he needed or desired. He began his investigation with a call to Philadelphia General where she had been taken after her first attack. She was there and had regained consciousness. He went straight to 10th Street to get Regina and then directed toward the hospital. On the drive there, William asked Regina several times what happened the night the police were called. Her short and direct answer left him to believe more had transpired than actually was told.

"Why is Mom in the hospital, Regina?"

"She fell down the steps," she answered again.

"Which steps? There are two sets of them." William found his patience getting short.

"I don't know." The child was irritated by the line of questioning which forced her to hold back the truth.

They reached the hospital and stopped at the information desk to find her room number. They took the elevator to the seventh floor to room 728. Regina's heart pounded as they approached the door and slowly opened it to find Carla barely recognizable. She had a black eye. Her head was bandaged. Her right cheek, upper lip and both knees bore stitches. Her right arm and her left ankle was broken. And her appearance was that of a horror flick monster as her face and head seemed twice its normal size from swelling.

"Mother, My God! What happened to you? And don't you dare tell me that a fall down a flight of stairs caused all of this!" William was furious.

"It's like Jay said. I fell down the steps at the apartment. I wasn't looking where I was going." Carla's dependence on Jay would not allow the truth to be known. He had waited until she awoke from the coma to coach her to corroborate his story.

William did not want to dispute his mother but he knew she was not being truthful with him. Therefore, he changed the subject. "How are you feeling? Are you in a lot of pain?"

"The nurse gave me some pain medicine a little while ago. I'm all right. I'll be fine," she struggled to persuade him.

The doctor came in to check his patient and William and Regina were asked to step outside the door.

"You can not convince me that a flight of stairs caused Mom to be all bruised and beaten this way, Regina."

She was already tired of reciting the same story and not remotely convincing a soul. So, she resorted to silence. She just wanted the whole nightmare to be long forgotten. She just wanted to erase those ghastly images of that night out of her mind. Instead though, they became just another something under the family rug to make the pile of dirt underneath more noticeable. She relied on what always worked to get her through yet another traumatic experience; a good attitude.

The doctor stepped out of the room and closed the door behind him. William stared at him intently. "What really happened to my mother."

"She and her husband says she fell down stairs. But, her injuries were caused by continuous blows with a blunt object. Luckily, there is no internal bleeding and miraculously no brain damage. Aside from being weak from excessive blood loss and extreme pain from her numerous injuries and broken bones, she will fully recover."

"What about her face?" William grimaced as he thought of it.

"Believe it or not, your mother's face and head have gone down considerably since she was brought in day before yesterday. Our first concern was the unconscious state in which the paramedics initially found her. Once she regained consciousness we asserted our attentions to her broken bones. We will just have to look at the options once the swelling has completely decreased."

"Thank you." William was appalled.

He went back in for a few minutes and Regina insisted she did not want to see her mother again until she was better. Her brave act would not go that far. In the car, on the long ride to West Philly, the overwhelming desire to know the truth about Carla's injuries plagued her brother.

"Regina?" He made eye contact for a brief moment and returned his eyes to the traffic of the street. "I'm going to ask you again. What happened to Mom? The doctor said that steps couldn't cause this. I want to know what happened, right now?" he asked in his most authoritative tone.

Regina felt trapped and divulged the accounts of that night. The recall of it brought back the hysteria as if the young girl traveled back in time just to suffer through the entire incident all over again.

"But, William you can't tell anybody because he said he would kill me if I told. He'll kill me!" she said. "He doesn't want to go to jail! He promised that he would kill me if I told what I saw!" she cried uncontrollably.

CHAPTER 19

Regina missed few days from school because the incident between her mother and stepfather took place over the weekend. William remembered how often Regina repeatedly switched from school to school over the last couple of years and voiced with his mother his concerns. They both agreed the child was better off with Lela so that her second grade year would not be interrupted as the first had been. But William was to pick her up on the weekends to relieve Lela of the responsibility of two children in her limited physical condition. Regina was never any trouble to her though because she knew how to clean up after herself and always did more than was required.

One weekend while Regina was with William, she asked to walk across the street to 68th and Ogontz to pay a visit to Geofreda who occupied the same little apartment that Malvin and Bernice resided in before the purchase of their current home. Even though she met the rest of her mother's children through William and his church, William and Geofreda were the ones she had a somewhat constant relationship with. Regina loved learning and Geofreda always had plenty of books, educational games and puzzles to play with obtained for her Special Education Curriculum even though she had no children outside of her school students. That particular Saturday afternoon, Geofreda read her Bible for several hours.

"What are you reading?" Regina was curious about what kept her sister's attention for so long.

"The Bible. Why are you hungry or something? Did you need for me to fix you something to eat?" Geofreda took very good care of Regina when she came to visit.

"No, not yet. I've been looking at you and you smile a lot when you read that book. It must be good? Every time I see you reading, you're always reading the same one." Regina failed to understand the difference between that book and any other.

Geofreda sat in the window sill reading by the day light. "Come over here and I'll try to explain this book to you. It's special. This book is about God and his son, Jesus. Now, there are different people in the book but they are the most important characters in all the different stories that are told. When I get upset about something I read this book because it makes me feel better and I can never stay sad for long. That's why I read the Bible so much."

"Who is God?" The child was most inquisitive.

Geofreda, gifted with the ability to wonderfully supply explanations so that even a child could gain an understanding, began. "God made the earth and all the people in it, Regina. God is a king. He lives in the sky above and the earth and we are here to make him happy by what we do for him," she said.

"Have I seen God?"

"No, I'm sure you haven't because God doesn't live on earth like we do. Remember I told you he lives in heaven in the sky. But when we talk to him, he can hear us."

"Who is God's parents and where are they?"

"God was always here. He is too big to have been born the way we were; with a mom and a dad. God was here first and everything else came because he made it. So, God doesn't need parents. Are you understanding what I'm telling you?"

"Yes, I like this story," Regina admitted.

"Some stories are true and some are make believe. The Bible is full of true stories, Regina. Now, because God loved us so much, he sent his son Jesus to come down to earth to live with us. It was hard for people to be good when they could not see God. And, he sent his son so that he could save us from the bad things that happen to us. He can make us feel better when we are sick or sad. Some bad people didn't like him and killed him. Now that he died and went back to live with his father, he talks to God for us. If we keep God and Jesus happy; he will keep us happy."

"Tell me again how I can make God and Jesus happy?" Regina wanted to know because she believed that she deserved to be happy.

"Talk to God and his son. God is our father and Jesus is our very best friend. When we talk to them, it's called prayer. When we thank them for what they do for us, it's called praise. And when we brag to God and Jesus about how good and strong they are, it's called worship. I know you don't fully understand but just talk to your invisible friend Jesus and God will be happy. That's how you keep them smiling down on you. Do you believe what I've told you? Because you must believe in God and Jesus in order for them to be your father and friend."

Regina closed her eyes tight and clasped her hands together like she had seen Geofreda and the people at church. She immediately talked to God.

"I believe in you God and Jesus. I really do believe. Please be my friend from now on. I want to be happy and I want to make you happy," she prayed. "I need a father, God. My father, Joseph, doesn't like me but, I'll be good for you so you can like me."

Geofreda was amazed at how quickly Regina learned and understood. The more questions that were answered for her, the more questions she issued. Geofreda and Regina stayed up all night talking and when the sun rose the next morning, the youngster had a warm, good feeling about her that she had never felt before.

"Geofreda I feel real happy inside already!" she said with excitement.

"Whenever you want that feeling again, you just talk to Jesus and he will tell our father, God, for you. You can tell Jesus anything. He will always listen and he will always care for you. Even when you are not such a good girl, he will love you anyway. Just because you believe in him, that makes him happy."

Her entire existence, Regina always felt the extreme pressures and weights of life. She forced herself to feel happy by putting the horrors of her mortality out of her mind. She never believed as though she belonged anywhere because as soon as she adjusted to a situation, the situation always managed to quickly evolve into something else. She was sure of nothing. She just traveled through the motions of life and merely survived through whatever means necessary. The means she found most successful was to just block tragedy from her mind. The next weekend with William, at his church, she finally understood what the people there were doing and she joined in with her whole heart to find Geofreda was right. That good feeling did return time and time again. For the remaining six weekends with her brother, she enjoyed church services and worshipped once or twice with Geofreda as well.

Carla was due to have her casts removed from her arm and ankle the following week and wanted Regina home with her. The child was extremely responsible for her age and practically cared for herself outside of preparing major meals, so her return would actually be to her mother's advantage. Regina had anxiously anticipated the return home but she wondered if Jay would be there.

"Did William tell the police and now Daddy Jay knows that I told what he did?"

Fear struck a deep cord in her and held a paralyzing grip. The first few days, Carla and Regina were alone. However, at night from the other side of the wall, Regina overheard conversations between Carla and Jay on the telephone. Jay was with his sister, Katherine.

"Jay, I know you didn't mean to hurt me. That's why I kept with your story that I fell down the steps. They told me they had evidence you beat me up. They tried to convince me to prosecute. But, I wouldn't break. I love you Jay and I know that you would never intentionally do anything to hurt me. It was the liquor. And now that you've explained to me how whiskey causes a chemical imbalance in your brain, we know that you can never drink again. That's all you have to do. Won't you please, come back home?"

Regina's heart sank, skipped a few beats and stopped for a moment because she somehow knew Jay would take the offer. Anger immediately replaced the fear.

"I saved her by running in the snow with no coat to get help. I didn't think about myself. All I could think about was her. She could have died because of what he did and I could have died trying to get help for her. And she wants him back? I'll tell her tomorrow how he told me he would kill me if I told anybody. I'll explain how, the snow kept going into my dress shoes and made my feet soaked and cold. She doesn't know how hard the wind was blowing and I couldn't breathe but, I kept on running for help. My lungs felt so heavy but, I couldn't stop running because I couldn't stop thinking about the way I saw her right before I left. If she knew what I saw she wouldn't want him back then. Yeah, I'll tell her how scared I was for her and for me because I told William what really happened that night. She loves me and she won't want him anymore after I tell her," she tried feverishly to convince herself.

CHAPTER 20

"**M**ommy, do you still want Daddy Jay to come home after all the things that I told you he said and what I saw him do to you?" Regina was determined to know.

"Regina, you know how Jay is when he drinks. He didn't mean to hurt me. He didn't even mean what he said to you. It was the liquor talking, not him. You know that he would never hurt you. He's always treated you like his daughter. He loves you!" She had minimized another situation because she desperately wanted Jay's love.

"You didn't see how he looked at me when he dared me to tell anyone what he did to you. You didn't feel how tight he held on to me to keep me from telling the police what really happened. You didn't see! You didn't see!" She screamed as tears rolled down her face.

"She's not going to listen to me. She didn't listen to me about Malvin and she didn't tell Aunt Pauline and Dena that she knew the truth. And now she acts like Daddy Jay beating her was no big deal. But, all those things..... they were a big deal. I know they were; or at least to me. Don't I matter at all? What about what I feel? What about what I want?" she thought to herself. Regina was angry, confused and afraid.

It took minimal effort. Jay was convinced that Carla would not prosecute him for beating her nearly to death with the iron pipe. He never wanted to feel the fear of imprisonment for his unruly behavior ever again.

"Carla, I promise I will never take another drink for as long as I live. I swear to you. My drinking nearly cost me my freedom and my wife. You won't regret taking me back. I promise!" Jay convinced himself and therefore was able to persuade his wife that her worries regarding his drinking was over. Regina stayed on her cot in the kitchen and just listened. She was not remotely satisfied with his smooth words.

"Regina, what are you doing in there. Don't you hear your Daddy's home. Come and give me a hug." Jay wanted to test the strength of the fear he had planted in her two months earlier. But, the street wise, little city girl was smart. She immediately showed herself in the doorway between the kitchen and the room where her parents talked.

"I can't let him know that I'm mad at him. I'll just act like nothing ever happened," she told herself.

"Hi, Daddy." She tried exceptionally hard to sound excited and did.

"Girl, you are getting so big. Come on and give me my hug," as he extended his arms to greet the child.

There was no hesitation in her movement into position to give the largest embrace that her little arms could manage. She refused to let him or anyone know how much she opposed his undeserved come back into her life. In her small mind, it was just better forgotten. Forgive and forget is what her mother told her to do. She was now a pro at it.

"That's my girl. Hey, let's walk to the corner store and get you some candy. I'm so proud of how brave you were for your mother the night she fell. You deserve a reward."

Regina never responded but gathered her jacket to walk with Jay. As they headed toward the door, Regina looked at Carla who wore the most glorious smile on her face. The trip to retrieve the treats seemed much longer than usual and Jay held her little hand and talked about all the wonderful things he wanted to do for her. She just listened and plastered a smirk on her face as imitation evidence that she was pleased with his conversation.

That night when she retreated to her cot, all she remembered was the mind boggling events of two months prior and his threat played over and over in her mind. Her heart beat was so rapid and as much as she wanted to sleep, she failed. Each time a rat ran across the floor of the dark kitchen, she would sit up with the expectation of Jay standing directly over her. When she had lain back down, the cycle repeated continually all night long. By the third night, Regina was more than angry with her mother. She was resentful because she no longer felt comfortable in the little apartment which had been home for the last few years.

"Hello Jesus," she whispered as she lay looking up at the ceiling. "I don't want to be scared to go to sleep any more. I'm so sleepy and I feel like my heart is going to run away from me, it is going so fast. Please pray to God for me so I can go to sleep without being so scared. I'm glad that I have you for a friend. Geofreda said that you will listen to me whenever I talk. I hope you can hear me even if I whisper and in the middle of the night. I don't want Mommy and Daddy Jay to know that I'm still up. I was a good girl today. I did my homework and I helped Grandma, Lela, by cleaning up the bathroom. I hope that makes you happy, God. I want to be nice to Daddy Jay so he doesn't beat my mom up again. Help me not to still be mad at him. I love Mommy and I want her to be.........ha..ppy....." she drifted into a sound sleep. Unfortunately for her though, her reality was transferred even into her dreams.

"He's gonna get me!" she screamed as she awoke from the nightmare.

"What's the matter, Regina? Are you all right?" Jay asked as he flipped on the light switch and stood in the doorway.

She looked at him in sheer terror. "Oh, I just had a bad dream. I saw a monster. It was just a bad dream that's all." She prayed that he would not stay near her any longer than he had to and so, she smiled in hopes to encourage him to leave her alone.

"It was just a nightmare. There are no such things as monsters." Jay tried to soothe her fears yet he could not possibly do so, being that he was a monster in the child's mind.

CHAPTER 21

The snow began to melt and the girls went outside in Darla's backyard in attempts to catch a stray cat that had climbed the fence in search for food. They dressed warmly and set out to make a pet of the feline which had wandered onto the property. Darla slipped and fell on something still hidden by snow and found it was the iron pipe that Jay used to beat Carla with some months ago. Along with it, bloody towels and clothing were discovered. In his efforts to clean up the blood and get rid of the weapon, he obviously opened the second story window of the kitchen and threw the clothing and pipe to be concealed in Lela's yard. He knew she was an amputee and the likelihood of her ever discovering the items was next to impossible. But, he failed to think the children would one day literally stumble upon it.

Jay stopped drinking completely for a while but soon befriended the man who lived on the third floor whose daily consumption was a norm. David rented the entire third level. The extra expenditure was prompted by his determination not to share a bathroom with anyone. He stayed to himself, spoke politely if he met anyone in the hall but always reported directly up the staircase located by Carla's apartment door. At first, Carla welcomed the development of a friendship with another male. Jay had been a loner except for his new found family and his sister, Katherine. It was healthy for him to bond with another man, or at least that was the initial feeling. After work, Jay came in, ate dinner, smoked a cigar and headed up to David's when he heard his footsteps on the steps leading to the level above. What started out as Friday night get-togethers soon became mandatory nightly meetings and Jay camouflaged his alcoholic breath with mints and gum upon returning home. Carla had a keen sense of smell though and easily distinguished the distinctive odor.

"Jay, you promised me you wouldn't drink anymore after what happened the last time. I'll leave you! I will! You think you can sneak upstairs without me knowing but, I can smell it. I'm not going through this with you anymore. You nearly killed me! If you continue to drink, you will come home to an empty house. I mean it, Jay!"

"Awe, woman, I only had a couple of beers. You know that liquor is my problem, not beer." Jay always had an answer for everything.

"I'm not even going to talk about this anymore. If you want to risk loosing your family over drinking, that's up to you." Carla dropped the subject as quickly as she had brought it up.

One Friday evening, Jay took his routine trip up to the third floor and visited for four hours. Carla heard the argument of the two from her apartment even with the door closed. Then, her ears witnessed the scuffle of feet, curses and objects fall to the floor. They fought until Carla dressed quickly, rushed up to the rescue and found that Jay was beating David with his fist.

"Jay, stop it, she yelled!" She dared not get in between two angry men. But, when her voice was heard, the fight stopped.

"You'd better get that crazy mother fucker out of my house before I kill his ass in here." David was furious as he touched his bottom lip to find the broken skin and blood.

"What did you say ass-hole? I don't give a God-damn who's damn house it is!" Jay stepped to brush past Carla as she latched onto his arm.

"Come on Jay, let's go!" Carla was not taking no for an answer. "What's the matter with you. I told you drinking was going to get your ass in trouble."

"I wasn't out of my head from drinking. I knew exactly what I was doing. He made rude comments about your butt to my face. He knows damn well you are my wife. He disrespected me as a man and as your husband. I'll kill any man about you, Carla. You don't do that shit! You don't talk about a man's wife's anatomy to his face!" Jay explained all the way back to their apartment.

She was relieved to know that liquor was not the culprit of this altercation. But, how could she be sure it had not been? She would just have to take his word for it. She had to believe in him. She could not rightfully accuse because there was the remote possibility that he was telling the truth. She chose to except his explanation.

Several hours later, Jay settled down to watch TV and Carla identified the smell of smoke. She first checked the stove because she knew Regina was in the kitchen alone. Jay then opened the apartment door to flames coming from a liquid filled bottle stuffed with an old rag soaked in gasoline. He quickly closed the door back and yelled to Carla to get buckets and the largest pots they owned and the containers were filled with water. He snatched a blanket from the bed and reopened the door to fight the flames. They had managed to double in size in no time at all and Carla found it necessary to open the door to the kitchen so she could have faster accessibility to water to fight the fire. Carla ceased water collection only to summon the fire department by phone and quickly began gathering again.

Jay noticed David peering from around the flight of steps which led to the first floor and he seized a large iron skillet Carla had placed on the stove. Jay chased the upstairs neighbor midway the steps and beat him with the frying pan.

Carla and Regina heard the echo of the skillet ring each time it connected with David's head but, they were overwhelmed and busied with fighting the fire. The bottle exploded, the fire engulfed the doorway and progressed upward toward the third floor staircase.

"Jay, stop it! You're gonna kill him! Stop it, Jay!" That's all Carla screamed while she continued the attempted flame control.

When Jay heard the sirens of the fire truck he stopped his assault and kicked David, sailing 2/3 from the top of the second floor in mid air to the bottom of the staircase, to the first floor below. He then returned to help in the fire fight.

The firemen mistook David for an overly intoxicated drunkard who had failed to make his way home and pushed him aside in the dark hallway. They raced up the steps with their hose to successfully extinguish the fire. It took only a matter of minutes and then the inquiry began. One fireman called the paramedics when he realized the alcoholic he had found lying on the first floor actually was in need of medical attention.

"Can you tell me what happened?" The fireman asked as he directed the question to either one who could supply the most accurate response.

"That bastard and I got into a fight and a couple of hours later this bottle filled with a rag and gasoline was on fire in front of our door. I caught him smiling and peeping at us under the staircase over there," Jay was happy to tell the fireman.

"It was good that you found it early and had the intuition to fight it yourself before we got here. You were very lucky."

"We weren't lucky? That ass-hole is the lucky one. He's lucky I didn't kill his ass!" Jay was still furious.

"Mr. Wilson, I understand that you are angry but, I'm going to have to pretend that I didn't hear your last statement. I'm going to have to ask you to calm down."

Carla whispered, "Jay, your mouth is going to write a bill that your ass can't pay. Just be quiet!"

The police came and Jay explained again what took place. Only this time, he was handcuffed and escorted away in the police squad car. David was taken to the hospital. Carla called Lela and rehashed the entire incident even though Regina frowned as her mother narrated by phone the entire situation in vivid detail, blow by vicious blow. She felt that she had seen quite enough for one day ......actually for a lifetime.

CHAPTER 22

C arla obtained no bail money for Jay nor did Katherine. The best that could be done was to wait on Jay's next paycheck which was due in on Friday. Carla called and visited daily and encouraged her husband to keep his spirits up in spite of his rather dismal situation.

"I'll loose my job if I don't report for work, Carla. You'll have to call my boss and tell him I'm sick......tell him anything but, make it good."

When the hearing finally took place, it was determined that Jay acted out of provocation and in self-defense for his family. When he returned home, the burned section of his doorway and corner was a constant reminder of what transpired and the mandatory time he spent incarcerated.

"Carla, we've got to get out of this rat hole. We need a house where no one can be responsible for our safety and well-being but us. My next paycheck will be a deposit for a house so you need to start looking somewhere near here so that Regina can stay in the same school."

The place she found was nothing fancy, but, it was clean and well kept by the landlord. Mr. Hill once lived in the row house at 2526 Warnock Street himself and kept it as a rental property once he moved to the suburbs. It was two stories with two entrances. It even had a little foyer to separate the front entrance from the living room. The backyard was fenced with 3/4 wood and the abandoned house adjacent to the left of the home could be viewed through the 1/4 chain link portion of the divider. The padlocked wooden gate allowed access to the alley directly behind the fence, not that anyone would possibly desire travel through those garbage infested trails. The outside wall of the kitchen and back entrance was beige stucco, contrast to the rest of the house which was deep red brick trimmed with dark brown paint. And there were several old oak trees for shade. It was so different from what Regina was accustomed to, however, and she thought her family had become somewhat wealthier because of the change in environment. The transition was definitely considered a move up from 10th Street yet, the reputation of the neighborhood was just as notorious. All the same, it was a single family dwelling and that was what mattered most.

Carla went over to the apartment to leave it spotless before she turned in the keys to the landlord, Ms. Tex, for the last time. She had just closed the door behind her as a middle-aged woman came from the third floor apartment with a box full of items.

"Hi Miss. I don't mean to disturb you," Carla said. "I am sorry about what happened to David. Can you tell me how he's doing? I hope he's doing better?"

"What is your name?" the woman inquired.

"Carla. I really feel bad about what happened to him."

"Well, thank you. My brother has recovered as much as one can who suffered brain damage and he's no longer able to live on his own. I'm here to pack his things so the apartment can be re-rented. He will have to stay with me so I can take care of him and these are the last of his things," she replied as she stared down into the box.

"It was nice of you to ask about him."

Carla was convinced his sister was unaware of who she was. She was equally sure her reaction would have been different if she had knowledge that Carla's husband caused her brother's condition. The whole situation made her extremely eerie and she found herself trying to get away without discovery as though she was a guilty criminal.

Six months went by and all was well with the Wilson family. There was no violence, no drinking and harmony seemed to replace such things. It took a considerable amount of pretense however, for Jay's irritability to be masked at home which was easily unleashed on strangers. Carla and Jay's association with their neighbors consisted of nothing other than a greeting in passing. Jay would totally ignore an older gentleman who sat on the front steps of his house as Jay headed home each evening. He always seemed intoxicated and the screen door behind him revealed the sounds of loud laughter, talking and the smell of several different brands of tobacco smoke. One evening, Mr. Mullis leaned forward as Jay walked by.

"Hay, can you give me a light?" He revealed to Jay his unlit, previously used cigarette.

"I don't have no God-damn light!" Jay snapped as he never missed a beat in his stride.

Some time later, Mr. Mullis became so overcome from his intake of liquor until he fell off the steps onto the hard cement pavement and the fall caused injury to his head. Jay heard him call for help from the corner and he knew there was no way the old man could not be heard by those just inside his house. When he reached him, Jay helped Mr. Mullis to his feet and called inside for assistance. Mrs. Mullis came to the door only because she heard an unfamiliar voice and was curious as to who showed her drunk, invalid of a husband any attention.

She was dark complexioned with completely gray hair. She always wore it in a French bun in the back of her head and her bang appeared as though she had just rolled out of bed. She showcased a huge mole on the left cheek of her face with two gray hairs which protruded from it. Even her nose hair which extended beyond her nostrils was gray. She had piercing coal black eyes, wore small-framed reading glasses on the end of her nose and spoke with a tone of voice that could have been easily mistaken for a man's. Her normal rate of speech was rapid and abrupt.

"Hey, fella what you doin'? He ain't got no damn money! What you tryin' to do, pick his pocket?" She stared at Jay through the screen door.

"Shit, your ass is ugly!" That statement slipped out of Jay's mouth unintentionally.

"Who the hell you callin' ugly? Your ass ain't so pretty yourself, you black bastard!" She was quick on her feet with insults because she practiced daily on those who came to gamble in her house or to buy liquor. Such language was common and required little of her emotion.

Jay was shocked at such a nasty mouth even for a woman with the appearance of Nosey Mullis. "I'm not trying to steal from him. Can't you see that he fell off the steps and hit his head?"

"Well, shit then! Why didn't you just say so in the first God-damned place!" She opened and extended the screen door so Jay could assist him inside.

"Hey, one of you men want to give me a hand with him?" Jay directed his voice toward the two men inside.

He laid Mr. Mullis on the sofa which reeked of urine. Matter of fact, the whole house smelled like a combination of urine, years of old smoke, alcohol and sex. Nosey returned to her card game even before Jay had actually placed her husband down.

"This man needs a doctor," Jay told the old woman.

"Hell, his ass falls all the time, he had a stroke and can't feel nothin' on one side. He'll be all right. Just give him a stiff drink of liquor, he'll feel no pain. What's your name stranger?"

"Jay," he answered. "Why are you giving him liquor if he had a stroke?" he pointed out while he headed for the door.

"Mind your damn business!" she snapped. "But, helpin' Mullis was decent of you. Sit over here and have a beer." Nosey pointed to an empty chair next to her.

"No. I really must get home to my family but, thanks anyway." Jay hurried out of the door. He was not worried about the temptation of a drink; he could no longer tolerate the rancid smell.

Nosey Mullis became a daily stop for Jay after that first initial meeting. He would not dare take a drink in such filth but, he would buy a beer and have it already open and in hand when he arrived for the visit. He spent hours refereeing the card games and fights that broke out and he would just barely escape before the police arrived. Dodging the police seemed to be a game Jay enjoyed. Carla noticed how with each passing day, Jay became later returning home from work. She also smelled the beer on his breath even though he had gone through nearly a whole pack of chewing gum to disguise his return to alcohol.

Carla befriended Mrs. Mullis' neighbor, Helena Garrison, who disclosed to Carla where her husband's afternoons were spent. She and the elderly woman set a trap for Jay the following week and Carla stood inside Helena's foyer until she heard Jay's voice as he exited the Mullis house. The minute he stepped out, Carla made her presence known.

"What the hell are you doing sneaking up on me?" Jay was totally surprised.

"I knew you were drinking, but I didn't know that you were hanging out in this whorehouse!" Carla furiously exclaimed.

Regina was at home alone. All Carla mentioned before she left was that she would be right back. Some time had expired since then and the child unlocked the screen door and looked in the direction of the route her mother had last traveled. There she heard all the commotion, cursing and saw a large group of people which included her mother and stepfather. She rushed up the street and experienced the vulgarity first hand. Carla noticed Regina yet did not give enough attention to want to stop her current behavior in the company of her daughter.

"Who does this bitch think she is? She walks these streets like she's the damn Queen of Sheba or some shit!" Nosey was fuming.

"Did that ugly ass bear call my wife a bitch?" Jay turned quickly to defend Carla.

"Helena started this whole shit. She needs to carry her old ass back in the house and mind her own damn business." Nosey pointed to her neighbor.

"You leave her out of it!" Carla was grateful to Helena for letting her in on her husband's well kept secret.

"All of yawl can kiss my black ass! Nosy turned her rear to the crowd, pulled her house dress up above her waste and flashed her torn underwear, in the middle of Warnock Street. The tear was of such extremity, her vagina and gray pubic hair was clearly visible to all. Everyone at that point, no longer held anger and laughter quickly replaced the emotion. But the most disgraceful action was not Ms. Mullis showing of her undergarment; it was the fact that no one even thought of the effects of the exposure the eight year old youngster had just experienced.

CHAPTER 23

" Jay, I would rather you keep your promise to me. But, if you insist on drinking, I would prefer that you do it at home. At least I'll know how much and what you drink." Carla knew in her heart that the smarter thing to do was to leave him. But, she desired not to do without Jay in spite of the occasional insanity which showed itself when he drank whiskey. This was just the welcomed invitation her husband needed to go back to his old ways. She was determined she would not condone his behavior by participating with him and this subject alone caused friction between the two of them.

It was Saturday afternoon and Jay went out to return with two quart bottles of Miller beer.

"What's the fun of drinking at home if I'm drinking alone?" Jay was insistent that Carla participate in his indulgence.

His wife wanted to ward off a probable argument before it was fueled so she took the bottle of beer, opened it, took a large gulp and detested its taste. She sat on one end of the long dining room table and Jay sat at the other.

"Hey, are you going to finish that beer or are you just going to play with it?" He quickly inhaled his quart and demanded some of the one he had purchased for his wife's pleasure.

"Yes, I want it but, I'm not in any great big hurry to drink it. Why?" Carla knew the reason he had asked but decided to portray ignorance.

"Because if you're going to waste perfectly good beer, I would rather drink it," Jay rationalized. "You've been holding on to it for nearly an hour. Just turn the damn thing up and drink it for Christ's sake!"

"Didn't you buy this beer for me?" Carla was irritated.

"Yeah, but you're not drinking it. You're playing with it and teasing me."

"I didn't know that my beer was that tempting to you, Jay."

"Then if you're not teasing me, just turn the fuckin' beer up and drink it!"

"I'm a grown woman. You can't tell me how to drink my beer. Are you crazy?"

Jay threw his empty quart bottle straight at Carla and it just missed her head by inches when it hit the wood paneled wall behind her, broke, splattered and slid down the wall. Carla had made up her mind that if she was going to remain with Jay despite his return to alcohol, it would be of the utmost importance to always have her wits about her and placement of herself in a vulnerable position by drinking until intoxication could never happen again.

When the bottle whistled past her head, her first instinct caused her to leap into action and she dove on Jay and choked him. The element of surprise gave her time to weaken an already unsteady opponent. He fell back in the chair to the floor and she sat on his chest with all her weight as she strangled the very life out of him. She then positioned one knee to intentionally connect on contact with his testicles. Now, he was breath deprived for three reasons. She had a choke hold on him. She had gained quite a bit of weight and all 200 lbs. of her cut off wind to his lungs. And lastly, the injury to his private area alone was enough to stop an elephant in its tracks.

Carla saw his eyes bulge and hoped she had not killed him. She let her anger and fear drive her to planned attacks of immediate defense the minute the situation called for it. Carla lifted herself off of his chest and loosed the grip around his neck. That instant air intake propelled Jay to jump up and run. He headed for the kitchen and Carla gave no opportunity for him to gain a weapon because she knew she controlled the fight if it remained fair. Her life depended on the battle only consisting of fists. She leaped on his back and held on with her forearm tightly under his neck, regaining her choke hold from the rear.

He struggled to shake her off and turned backwards suddenly as he slammed her back up against the kitchen wall. He tried his counter move several times before Carla dug her fingernails deep into Jay's neck. Between the pain from the scratches and the sweat seeping into the broken skin, he was miserable. Jay reached the backdoor. He knew if he could enter the backyard, his new iron plumbing pipe that he kept outside would control the woman whom had turned the attack back on him. He thought he had it hidden well out there. But Carla watched him closely and vowed he would never be given the chance to use his advantage again. She was aware of the pipe's existence and had not discarded it merely to keep Jay from knowing she had an awareness of his secret. They fell through the screen door onto the pavement and Carla lost her hold on Jay's shoulders. She took her fingers and dug into both nostrils as he fell up against the stucco wall. His shirt was ripped from his back and Carla persistently reeked havoc with his sinuses. He slid for a short distance down the wall which caused deep gashes in his back. Again, the sweat which escaped from his pores stung in the fresh wounds from the stucco. He was in agony and weakened.

Regina overheard Carla talking about the newly wrapped pipe she found to Helena one afternoon. Now, her parents were in the yard where it was said to have been kept, the child's mind flashed back to the memories of Carla when she was beaten bloody and unconscious. She immediately ran out the front door. Germantown Avenue was a savior that winter night of the first marital fight and

Regina needed a savior once more. It was a shorter distance than before and the warmth of the summer made the run less taxing on her lungs. The squad car pulled up to the curb of the house and as before, Regina ran inside with two officers in close pursuit. When she entered, both parents were seated where they had been originally before the entire incident began. Both were sweating profusely and Jay's blood penetrated through the fresh clean shirt he had obviously most recently put on.

"Miss, is everything all right?" The officer directed his question to Carla because her hair was in total disarray.

"Yes officer, everything is fine," she answered as she tried to give a smile.

The officer looked at Jay who had plainly gotten the worst end of the deal and repeated the question.

"Yes, you heard the lady. Everything here is fine," he managed to get out in between the deep breaths of exhaustion.

The police viewed the house which showed evidence of some type of domestic situation but, with neither party admitting a problem; there really was no report to be made.

"Miss, if you have any problems, you just give us a call and we'll come back." The police kept their attention directed toward Jay.

"Thank you officers but, I'm sure I'll be fine," Carla was confident.

Carla had reached the pipe before Jay could get to it and tossed it across the fence into the alley. The door to the gate had been previously padlocked for added security and the key was indoors. Once Jay saw that his goal would not be met, he surrendered. The fight was over.

Carla came in calling to Regina and assumed she heard the chaos and went for assistance. They then scrambled to return the house to some normalcy before Regina's return with police.

"Regina, why did you run out of here like that?" Carla was upset.

" I thought Daddy Jay was going to beat you up again and I went for help before it got really bad." Regina felt like one would feel if interrogated on the witness stand in court.

"You need to learn how to stay out of grown people's business. I don't need to answer to the police about what goes on in my house. I can handle my house. Do you hear me?"

"I got the police because I thought you were in trouble again," the child defended.

"Well as you can see, I wasn't the one you needed to save this time," and she looked at Jay with pride for her most recent victory.

Carla possessed new found confidence. But, she forgot about the state she ended up in the last time Regina found the need to involve the authorities. She possibly would not have survived if they had not intervened. Now, after her mother's scolding, Regina's whole perception of right and wrong was distorted and confused.

CHAPTER 24

Carla bragged to all her neighbors of her defeat of Jay that day. It was as though she managed to succeed some insurmountable climb and reached the very top to stake her claim. She was not aware that after his loss to her, Jay sought medical attention for shortness of breath and feelings of being light headed. He left as though he was determined for work but made an appointment for a physical examination. It was found through tests that he suffered various symptoms because his heart was in very poor condition. He was informed of the short length of time in which he had to live and the report automatically softened his usual abrasive behaviors. He stopped his alcohol consumption completely in hopes of reversing the inevitable and never told Carla of his illness. Within two months of his doctor's visit, Jay was found dead on the trolley on his way to work.

Regina was dressed and prepared to start her daily journey for school when Carla gave her the news of her stepfather's departure from life. Unfortunately, the child did not truly have a realistic view of death. Her knowledge of it was limited and she failed to understand that death was possible without some sort of trauma triggering a person's demise. She was not aware of death by natural causes.

All of Carla's children were notified. Geofreda came over to her mother's house in order to provide some comfort and assistance during a difficult time. She had met Jay once or twice and loved his eccentric sense of humor. She, as did her mother, enjoyed the laughter. She also loved his intellect and found him to be extremely bright and witty in spite of his lack of formal education.

Pauline put aside her differences for the dismal occasion to show support for her sister. Angel, Patsy, Geofreda, Katherine, Annabelle and several other family, friends and neighbors came for the wake the night before the funeral. The ceremony was to take place the following day at 11:00 a.m. and the hour was getting late.

"Regina, it's time for you to get ready for bed. You will have to get an early start tomorrow and you'll need to get as much sleep as possible," Carla instructed.

"Mommy, can I stay up just a little while longer? I promise I will not give you any trouble tomorrow when it's time to get up."

Regina was afraid to go to the second level of the house alone. She assumed since she had overheard that Jay's spirit would always be with them; he could somehow know her current feelings about him. She was relieved and even glad that he was dead. She no longer had to worry about him finding out that she revealed his secret about beating Carla nearly to death. She also realized that his death removed the threat of him ever being able to harm her and the truth was now free to come out. She no longer had to listen and then investigate to see to her mother's safety. There was no more need for the youngster to race home from school just to make sure she arrived home before Jay in case of an incident. Yes, she was relieved and even happy he was no longer in her life and felt no guilt about the love/hate emotions she possessed for him.

Regina's mind drifted back to two nights prior to Jay's death when she was awakened by the sound of moaning at 2:00 a.m. from a sound sleep. Her immediate fear was that she had slept through a disagreement and her mother had been injured or surprise attacked while she slumbered. The child crept down the hall to a partially opened door and veered through the separation of the door hinges and frame to see the silhouette of her parents engaged in intercourse. She really had no understanding of what was taking place but she was smart enough to differentiate between the moans of pleasure and pain. The threat of violence was gone now, along with the man who brought so much injury to both she and her mother.

"Didn't Mom tell you to go take your bath and get ready for bed?" Geofreda was surprised that her sister had not yet ventured up the long staircase because Regina usually obeyed the instant instructions were dispersed.

"OK," she replied.

But, she procrastinated cleaning up her toys so as to prolong the time. She felt for the light switch in the bathroom which was located directly in front of the staircase, she filled the tub, closed the door, undressed and entered the bath water. It was so quiet upstairs and she envisioned the doorknob slowing turning to find Jay standing there looking at her with vengeance in his eyes. Her imagination gained the better of her and she quickly splashed water on herself, dressed in her night gown and returned to the company of her family below.

"Child, there is no way you took a bath that fast," Carla stated.

"I did Mommy. I washed up really fast but I did a good job." The child failed to convince her mother or any other person in the room.

"You couldn't have taken a bath that quickly. Come here." Geofreda felt the child's skin and noticed most had not been touched by water, nor was there any smell of soap. "Go right back upstairs and take a bath like you've been told!"

Regina returned to the bathroom and repeated the earlier steps. This time she left the door open and sat in the tub for an additional five minute. The darkness of the hall made the anticipation of seeing Jay much more intense and she hurried to return to her family once again.

"Girl, what is wrong with you? You have never given anyone this much trouble and you normally love taking baths." Carla was baffled.

"Regina, now you know that Daddy Jay was a very clean man. If you don't get upstairs and bathe yourself good, he's going to sit up in his casket at you tomorrow," Geofreda suggested.

She returned to the bathroom once more to bathe. As she sat in the tub, she began to talk to her friend, Jesus. "In church they said I shouldn't be afraid of anything if I believe in you. Jesus, I am so scared up here by myself. Please, don't let Daddy Jay get me? Please, don't let his spirit be mad at me?" Not only did she bathe, she scrubbed her skin until it was red and irritated to insure a thorough cleansing. She finished and returned downstairs.

"Regina, the reason you had to take your bath was so you could go to bed. What are you doing back down here?" Carla was irritated, now.

"Geofreda will you talk to me before I go to sleep?" Regina wanted everyone to think that she was brave and therefore, failed to give admittance to her fears.

"Yes, come on. I'll walk you up to bed," Geofreda responded as she got up to hold the small hand of the eight year old.

CHAPTER 25

The services began on time in the little funeral home on 2nd Street. As the family entered, they viewed Jay's remains lying directly in front of them in a steel gray casket. Carla held Regina by the hand and started toward the deceased. Regina's heart beat was so rapid until she believed it possible that it may leave her body.

"Oh, no! I don't want to go near him. He might know that I was happy about him being dead and get me," she thought to herself.

"Jay is dead and he can not harm you or threaten you any more," the soothing voice inside said to her reassuringly.

She still found it necessary to hold her breath as her mother stood in front of the casket looking down into the face of the man she had shared her life with and loved for four years. She and her mother sat on the front row and the actual eulogy began. Kind words were spoken about Jay but, Regina heard nothing of all the fights and the anger that came up when he drank. She did not recognize whom they were speaking of as the man she had known as Daddy Jay.

Suddenly, it struck her. "Oh God! I can't remember whether I washed behind my ears last night! He's going to sit up at me to check my ears! Did I? Didn't I? Oh Lord, help me!" She breathed erratically and when she noticed Carla was trying to take her nearer to her stepfather's body for the final viewing, Regina resisted. She struggled with all her strength while she whaled hysterically. No one could understand what was being said and most interpreted her actions as extreme grief. Carla pulled her even closer for comfort and it was more than the young girl could handle. Regina's imagination caused her eyes to see Jay's body sit up to stare straight at her and she collapsed right there on the spot.

"Jay must have been really good to that child for her to take his funeral so hard," said his sister, Katherine.

"Yes, he was good to her," Carla agreed.

Pauline stared at Regina with a look of discontent. "That girl is such an actress. She will do or say anything to get some attention."

Regina remained in the car with Geofreda while the others went graveside to deposit Jay Wilson in his final resting place. She had noticed her aunt's distrustful looks since the night before during the wake.

"She hates me for telling on Dena. She'll always hate me," she fought with herself as if the events of the day alone had not been taxing enough.

"You really loved him didn't you?" Geofreda asked as she noticed Regina's attentions fixed on the crowd around the grave site.

"I can't let her know that I hated him," she thought and then responded. "Yes, he was more like a father than I have ever had." She did not lie, exactly.

After the cemetery, everyone returned to Carla's home and there was food and refreshments everywhere. All the mourners gathered at the house to continue to provide support and comfort for the new widow. They told the jokes Jay had shared and also talked about his fights and temper. The man the family now described was the one Regina remembered.

Around 7:45 p.m. the crowd thinned and Carla and Regina cleaned to burn the nervous energy that still existed in excess for them both. The restoration of the house to its original state had been completed, all except Jay's presence. It felt strange to have peace and quiet but, both were a welcomed change for Regina. Carla, on the other hand, seemed disturbed by her new found freedom and the calm that it brought to her life. It was as though she was so accustomed to major events happening daily until the absence of drama meant life was somehow missing excitement. She was uncomfortable and she could only find solace in Jay's old hang-outs.

"I'll be right back, Regina. I'm going up to Mrs. Mullis' for a minute."

She walked up the street. She stepped up and rang the doorbell to find the place crowded and smoke filled as usual. Jay's lifestyle was much more inviting to her now that he was gone.

"Hey, Mrs. Mullis. Can I come in?" Carla was not sure whether their last encounter would permit her visit to be accepted.

"I heard about Jay. You come on in here and have a drink on me." Nosey knew if she could successfully encourage Carla to drink, it would not take much coercion to have her gamble and prostitution would be next on the agenda.

"I can get good money for this one. She's nice looking and hurting still," she thought.

Carla had two drinks and found the existing card game of Pity Pat to be too irresistible. The more she drank, the more she gambled. The more she gambled, the more she drank. Three hours had gone by since she left home that evening. Regina was worried and was also afraid of being alone in the multi-level house. She reached for the keys which were kept in a bowl in the china cabinet, locked the front doors and proceeded to the Mullis house.

"Is my mother here?" Regina peered past the strange man who opened the door to hear Carla's laughter as she won the hand of cards.

"Who is your mother?" asked the stranger.

"She's right there," she said as she pulled the screen door with her little fingers and opened it to enter. She went over to Carla's side and stood near her before she was noticed.

"What are you doing here? I told you I would be right back. Why didn't you stay home like I told you to?" Carla's focus was still on the card game that had just begun. She also accepted a cigarette offered by one of the other players which Regina had never seen her do.

"I was scared that something bad happened to you and I didn't like being down there by myself," Regina explained.

"OK. You can stay here but you've got to get out of the way." Carla feared that her winning streak would be interrupted.

Nosey, turned on the black and white television located in a corner of her cluttered and untidy living room. American Band Stand was the programming of choice for Nosey and Regina was attracted to the lively music. She stood in front of the TV and watched all those young people dance. She recognized within a few minutes that she could duplicate their movements to the letter and enjoyed the generated attention.

"I like dancing," she told herself. But a strong guilt came immediately and she struggled within herself between what the voice inside was telling her and her desire. "I'll just do it this once and I won't do it again. I can go back to being a good girl tomorrow."

CHAPTER 26

Regina began spending a large majority of time at Mrs. Mullis' and even returned from school there because her mother visited so frequently. She often found solace upstairs behind the closed door of Nosey's guest bedroom/storage room for the necessary quiet level in which to complete her homework. Concentration was difficult with all the vulgar language, the effects of excessive smoke on her eyes and men in their drunken stupor staring at her with sly grins. She also slept in that room when the hour got late and it was time to put herself to bed. She would rather be near her mother than down the street at their home alone all night.

Regina wondered how Mrs. Mullis survived. She never saw her turn in for the night. She witnessed her take little cat naps in between selling whiskey and gambling but that was the only rest ever observed. She drank and played cards all day and all night. Nosey, like her grandmother, was rumored to be a modern day witch.

Carla received Jay's Social Security and he had arranged for his stepdaughter to get monthly allotments as well. In all actuality, the Social Security exceeded that of what Jay's paychecks amounted to monthly. However, the more time she spent with Nosey, the less money she had for bills. And if gambling caused an arrears, Mrs. Mullis would gladly lend money so as to encourage more gambling. It was a vicious cycle and Carla soon found that it was extremely difficult to get off the merry go round. But, her sense of decency finally came to the rescue. Carla stood because she had nothing left of the borrowed money in which to play the next hand. Her limit had been reached. As sad as she was about it, her lack of finances excluded her from the next game.

"Carla, come in the kitchen with me a minute." Nosey had a plan.

"Yeah, what's wrong, Mrs. Mullis?" Carla was concerned because she had never been called aside before.

"I've got a way you can make quick money since you need some." Nosey was a little hesitant.

"How can I make more money? You want me to help you sell liquor or

91

something?" Carla asked naively.

"No." She pulled the indebted woman over to the kitchen door and pointed to a man at the table engrossed in the card game.

"Do you see that man right there? He will give you $300.00 to go to bed with him right now."

Carla's mouth flew open in total surprise and disgust. She had done many things that were considered immoral but that's where she drew the line.

"Have you lost your mind? I would never sleep with somebody for money. I don't care how much they offered me. You must be crazy?"

"Well, you've done everything else. Why not this?" Nosey was sure the need for money would overpower the repulsive suggestion.

Carla slapped Mrs. Mullis across the cheek, obtained her purse and yelled upstairs to her daughter.

"Regina, come on let's get the hell out of here!"

Regina was sound asleep and was not aroused until the third or fourth call. She gathered her books, slipped into her pants, and placed her feet into both her shoes. She failed to understand why her rest was disturbed in the middle of the night. Usually, she put herself to bed and woke in time to go to her house to bathe and dress for the new day before walking the seven blocks to school. That night was different and she staggered sleepily down the street with her mother at 2:00 a.m. destined for home.

"Don't bring your black ass to my house no God-damn more.....You'd better pay me back every sent of the money I lent you too!" Nosey yelled out the front door as the sound of her voice echoed in the early morning air.

Carla's disassociation with Mrs. Mullis did not cause her to resort to staying at home because she immediately replaced one gambling house with that of the next door neighbor, Helena Garrison. She passed right by Nosey's crowded, noisy dwelling with her nose turned up and entered the Garrison home to gamble, drink and do her usual cursing and smoking. Those activities seemed to be equivalent for her to the infatuation of an addict to drugs. It was in her blood. At 11:00 p.m., Regina noticed a pull out sofa bed unmade in the living room and did lay across the foot of it to rest her tired small body.

Regina's appetite was extremely suppressed and her lifestyle left her in a state of depression. Luckily for Carla, that posed an even better situation for less distractions. Milk and cereal and cream of wheat were usually kept at home so that when it came time for the child to dress, she prepared a quick breakfast for herself and after her school day was done, her new destination was the Garrison household once again.

That particular afternoon, the Garrison's neighbor, Gail, who lived to the left of them came over to play cards. Her daughter, Cookie, was sitting on Helena's front steps playing jacks. Regina was very good at the game due to the instructions during her brief friendship with her old neighbor, Darla, Hanna's grand-daughter, and (unhappily to say) her cousin, Dena. The card game took place in the dining room. And there was a long hallway that led past the dining room door to the front entrance.

"Mrs. Garrison, what's her name again?" Gail asked as she pointed to Carla.

"I'm Carla why do you ask?" she wondered.

"Ain't no way in hell that you can win six times in a row," the woman insisted.

"What are you trying to say, Gail?" Carla disliked the turn of the conversation.

"I ain't tryin' to say nothin'. I'm sayin' that you're cheating," Gail responded boldly.

"All right, Bitch! You don't know anything about me! I'd rather whip your big black ass than to sit here and let you call me a cheater."

"Well, let's just take it outside then." Gail was furious.

"You lead the way!" Carla insisted.

Gail stood up from the table and walked toward the doorway and Carla jumped her from behind just as she reached the hallway. They both landed on the floor. Gail was much heavier and Carla used the surprise attack in order to gain the upper hand. She pushed Gail's face to the floor repeatedly and they yelled and cursed each other profusely as they struggled to overtake one another. Gail never gained control and finally after the initial shock wore off, Mr. Garrison was able to separate both women. Mr. & Mrs. Garrison was adamant for Gail to leave their home. No matter what, Carla was their friend and an enemy of Carla's was their enemy also. Gail stepped outside the front door as she was escorted out by Mr. Garrison and found Regina and Cookie engaged in a brutal fist fight as well.

They had been startled by the loud lamentation and curse words of their parents and both peered through the storm door to find their mothers throwing punches like two men.

"Girl, you'd better get your mother off my mother's back!" Cookie was angry.

"I don't have anything to do with what is happening in there. Who do you think you're talking to anyway?" Regina was rather perturbed by the very suggestion of such.

"You heard what I said," as she came close in Regina's face only to be pushed backwards with such force that Cookie fell.

"Get up! I'll teach you about coming up in my face!" and Regina's fists began to fly.

Carla and Helena witnessed the commotion and loud voices as Mr. Garrison separated the two girls. Regina was more like her mother than she had imagined because she too had gotten the better of her opponent. Regina and Carla were both pushed into the house and Gail and Cookie were encouraged by Helena and George to go home.

CHAPTER 27

School was the most wonderful experience in the world for Regina. She loved the environment and found that her natural intellectual abilities brought about a tremendous amount of positive attention. The teachers found her to be a joy to teach and measured her growth by her desire to learn. To her, school was the one place where she could be herself and enjoy the fruits of her labor. There, the focus was on her and that she was not accustomed to.

Mrs. Swartz, the art teacher, announced an exciting new contest and Regina listened intently. "Today class, Clymer Elementary is holding an emblem contest for grades 3-6. You are to create a design which is to be displayed as our school patch to be worn on jackets, book bags or whatever you'd like to display your school spirit. Today is Monday. The contest ends on Friday. So, that does not give room for delay. You must present your finished patch to me by the end of class on Friday to have your entry submitted in the contest. The 1st place winner will receive an AM/FM portable radio, various art supplies and $25.00. The 2nd place winner will receive $10.00 and a sketch pad. The 3rd place winner will receive a water color set. Remember, the deadline is this Friday."

Regina needed to enter. Her heart beat rapidly and the excitement almost overwhelmed her. She rushed home from school to discuss the events with her mother. Carla was engrossed in her card game as usual but promised to hear all the details when the two returned home. It was 11:00 p.m. when Regina mustered up enough energy to fill her mother in on the contest which intrigued her so.

"Mom, the contest is for 3rd, 4th, 5th and 6th graders. I want to enter so bad but, the older kids will probably win." Regina's eyes were tired but yet still excited.

"It doesn't matter who else enters the contest. You just remember to do your very best and that will always be good enough, even if you don't win. Just do your best." That was the most motherly advice Carla had ever given and the most positive.

Regina retired for the night with the thoughts of the contest like visions of Christmas sugarplums dancing in her head. She hardly slept because of the anticipation of her design of the school patch for the following day. She arose early, dressed, ate a quick bowl of cereal and rushed to school. Her first class of the day was art and she hurriedly placed her books under her desk and went to work. She first created the shape of the patch and decided to use a circle. She then drew pieces of puzzles that were obviously a perfect fit but 1/2 inch spaces separated each piece. Then off to the left she drew a slightly curved line from the far top of the circle to the bottom and in that space wrote the school name downward. The puzzle pieces were colored red as well as the school name and the spaces in between and around "Clymer" remained white. It was beautiful and artistically creative. Very little thought went into the patch and therefore, she simply minimized its beauty and originality. Mrs. Swartz, walked around the classroom as the students worked feverishly on the patch project. She looked over Regina's shoulder and gave a broad smile but made no comment. But, Mrs. Swartz was amazed by the detail and the creativity behind the patch and knew that the judges would feel the same. Regina looked it over one last time before she entrusted it to the teacher.

"Regina, don't you want to work on it some more. You still have Wednesday through Friday to fully complete it." The teacher did not believe there was any more work necessary but, if the first emblem turned in was selected as the winning entry, this would cast suspicion with the other children. "Regina, just take a day or two to look it over and if you are still satisfied with your patch, then by all means, turn it in just as it is."

Regina was baffled. "Did Mrs. Swartz feel her patch was incomplete? Did she not like her creation? What else should or could be added?" These thoughts plagued her for two days and finally on Thursday after class, Regina turned in her patch. But, doubt set in and she quickly pushed the thoughts of the contest from her mind because she was convinced that she could not possibly win. The patches were judged on the following Monday and the winners were announced on Wednesday over the intercom during class.

"We are proud to announce the winner of our school patch design contest. All of the entries were wonderful but there could only be one winner. And what a beautiful patch we've chosen to be our school emblem. The 1st place winner of our 1st Emblem Contest is in our 3rd grade, Regina Ulzler." The announcement came and the child's heart literally stopped for a several seconds. She had won! She sat there in shock for a minute only to be brought back to reality by the cheers of her classmates. She did not even hear who was awarded as the 2nd and 3rd place winners.

"I can't believe I won! There were kids older than me who made patches. But, I won!" she told the young girl who shared a seat directly beside her. She loved the attention of her classmates and her teacher beamed with pride as she stretched out her arms to award Regina with a congratulatory hug.

"I'm so proud of you, Regina! I know your mother will be also. We will have an award ceremony on next Wednesday and I know you look forward to getting your prizes."

"I still can't believe I won, Ms. Swartz!" she replied in amazement.

Regina rushed home again that day. For once, she found her mother at home instead of the Garrison's which in itself was a pleasant surprise.

"Hey Mom! I won the contest! I won the patch contest!" she yelled as she entered the front door.

"I knew you could do it, Regina. I told you all you had to do was your best and that would always be good enough." Carla smiled with pride as she responded.

Then Regina's smile disappeared and sadness replaced it. "I sure wish my daddy could be at the awards ceremony. He probably won't come but, will you call him and ask him for me?" She was filled with skepticism but, was somewhat hopeful only because of her against the odds win.

"I can't promise you anything, Regina. I will call him, though." Carla really would have preferred not to be in contact with Joseph.

The emblem contest was the first time the underprivileged girl was able to taste sweet success. She loved the feeling and vowed to handle everything with the same "I can do it" attitude. She wanted that good feeling to never end and it replaced all the uncomfortable and painful situations she had encountered. She believed now she possessed the power to overcome and to take charge over every unfortunate thing that could ever happen to her. The contest gave her a sense of pride and accomplishment and left her wanting more out of life and to strive for only the best of what it had to offer.

The entire school participated in the awards ceremony. The winning emblem was converted from paper to an actual patch and each child received one for school spirit. Carla found herself in the large auditorium filled with elementary children for the first time since enrolling Regina in school. That was the only reason for the visit because the bright girl always made good grades and behaved like a perfect young lady. Regina was proud to have a reason to share her mother with her classmates. As she sat beside Carla filled with anxiety and happy thoughts, she wondered if her father had come and was somewhere in the midst of the crowd of people who were all there to pay tribute to her. She then heard her name called. She stood immediately and proudly walked from the back of the auditorium up the stairs to the stage in front of the entire school.

"Hello, Regina." The principal greeted her. "Congratulations. We are so proud of our new school emblem and we wanted to let everyone here at Clymer meet the creator of our patch. Did you want to say anything to your schoolmates?" He held the microphone to her small full lips.

"I didn't believe I could win because there were so many kids here and many were older than me. But, my mother told me to just do my very best and that would be enough even if I didn't win. She was right! My best was enough! Even enough to win. All I had to do was believe in myself and do my best."

"Well, your best was enough and here are the art supplies, $25.00 cash and the AM/FM radio you've won by your design of the Clymer Elementary School Emblem. I hope you will enjoy them."

"Thank you, Mr. Bryant," she said as her arms were loaded with the winnings.

"What did you say?" Principal Bryant had awarded the 3rd and 2nd prizes leading up to Regina and neither child had expressed appreciation. He found her response most refreshing.

"I just said thank you." Regina failed to see the significance because manners came so naturally to her.

"No, young lady, you did not just say thank you. Manners and a good attitude will take you farther in life than any talent alone can. I see you going far because you are pretty, smart, talented and you have a wonderful attitude. Let me see what else I can give you as a reward for that special quality." He reached into his pocket and gave her a crisp twenty dollar bill in addition to all she had just received.

A huge smile shown on her face and again she replied, "Thank you."

"Let's give Regina Ulzler a big hand of appreciation. I expect great things from this young lady."

As she returned to her seat, the roar of the crowd brought tears to her eyes and when she reached her mother's side once again she just sat in awe of all that had transpired. It was, by far, the most magnificent day of her life and she did not want it to ever end. She and Carla left for home together that day and nothing was said during the six block walk. Regina was not sure as to what was on her mother's mind. But, she found herself wondering whether Joseph bothered to show up. His presence would have been the icing on the cake. Unfortunately, there was no icing. But, she was definitely very grateful for the cake.

CHAPTER 28

The established church memories with Geofreda and William made Regina long for that lifestyle. She misinterpreted those feelings as being based on their economic standing, when in fact, it was the peace and serenity she coveted. She was forever on guard around the constant contact with strangers in which her mother determined to associate. She never knew what to expect and therefore, never slept sound or really relaxed. That was not the way a nine year old was designed to excel but that was the only existence there was for Regina. She often sat alone and wondered why some of her older siblings did not adopt to relieve Carla of her motherly responsibilities so that she could proceed with her life of gambling and booze without interruption. Most days the girl just wanted to be rescued by anyone and everyone. One day she managed to collect enough courage to ask her mother questions about her life choices for the two of them.

"Mom, why do you play cards and drink with those people?"

"That's just how I have my fun. Just like you enjoy playing jacks and jump rope, it's the same for me. Why do you ask?" Carla was shocked by the question which seemed to come completely unexpected.

"My life is so different from William's and the others. They don't do the same things that you do and I always like being with them and how they live. They don't play cards and drink. Why not?"

"That's just the kind of fun that I like but everyone doesn't like the same things, Regina." Carla became irritated and defensive.

"Can we go to church on Sundays like they do? I like going to church. It makes me feel good," the child explained.

Carla was at a loss for words. How could she argue with an innocent request such as going to church? Why had she not wanted to do so herself? She knew the time had come where she would have to place her daughter's well-being and welfare over her frivolous habits. Her conscience came to the forefront and led her to do the right thing for once.

"So, you like going to church?" She somehow hoped that the youngster had changed her mind since having asked the original question.

"Yes. The only thing I wish is that we would go together. Can we go this

Sunday?" The child was anxious.

"I'm not going on the trolley all the way over to William's or Geofreda's church. But since you are so determined, I will find a church for us to go to," Carla promised.

"You'll find it by this Sunday?" Regina was stern and would not leave any room for her mother to abandon the commitment.

"Yes! I said I would find one and I will." The pressure was on.

Carla had noticed a church sign many times in route to William and Geofreda's, located on the corner of Germantown and Lycoming Streets. She called to find out the times of services and gained the schedule of the trolley so that she could be on time.

Nazarene Baptist Church was a medium-sized church with angelic stained glass windows. Regina looked around in awe because she had never seen such a beautiful church. They attended for several months and to Carla's surprise, she lost the desire to drink or gamble. She replaced such activities with reading the Bible and being more of a homemaker. No, there was not the fast food in the refrigerator or a loving responsible male which was found at William's home but, there was now a calm over her household that had been unimaginable to her. A change had taken place in her mother's life. Carla actually looked forward to attending church and it was not just a means by which Regina could participate. They both enjoyed Sunday School and the services. Carla's lifestyle change was attributed to her youngest child even though her eldest son and daughter were more experienced and had tried unsuccessfully for many years.

Regina, for the first time in her life, knew security as Carla provided it. She lived from age nine through ten without any major incidents. But, because the beginning had been so dramatic for her, she subconsciously longed for action and adventure. She was bored and unimpressed by most television shows because she had seen much more graphic things in real life. Serenity was disturbing and it was inevitable for drama to return. As long as Carla was not faced with decisions of change, things were fine but new people entered her life and along with them came improper decisions made with the wrong motives.

Carla was informed by Pauline that their sister, Pansy, had been institutionalized due to a severe nervous breakdown. It seemed that the man whom she had fallen in love with, married and had four children with, just left her and the children without so much as a second thought. He moved in with a woman who was much less attractive and had even less going for her. The pressure of handling the four small children alone and constant worry over her husband's failure to return home proved to be more than she was equipped to handle. The children were separated so that there would not be such the burden with them all remaining together. The two boys ran away from home to live on their own as teenagers. The oldest daughter was sent to Pansy's brother, Lofton, to be raised with his two sons and the youngest daughter was shifted from one foster home to another. Carla allowed her guilt associated with the abandonment of her own seven children to cloud her judgment.

Carla traveled to Bridgeport, Connecticut and assessed the conditions of her niece, Elantra. She had no sense of belonging and manners where quite far removed at that point. She was a wild as an alley cat and street wise beyond her years. She was also a survivor and knew how to think only of herself and her needs. But, all Carla managed to see was a scared thirteen year old who had been shuffled from place to place, who needed a home and to be wanted. Because she was a blood relative, the state of Connecticut gave guardianship to Carla and Elantra was transported back to Philadelphia to live. She knew that no one else wanted her and she believed it hard to conceive that Carla was willing to care for her without ulterior motives. The former foster parents were only interested in the money they gained by providing a home and shelter. Carla saw an opportunity to prove that she was a good person after all.

Elantra was enrolled in school and Carla overcompensated for her niece's misfortunes by overlooking her own daughter's needs. They had just found a minute mother-daughter relationship through church that had not yet matured into what the average ten year old was due. Now, here was a third party to widen the gap that had just begun to be bridged. Everything was done to accommodate the new-comer. Things that were special for Regina were now overlooked because Carla was determined to make a young lady of her niece. It had become her passion to show everyone that she had the ability to transform a wild, untamed girl into a wonderful young woman. She refused to see that the very attentions that she directed to Elantra was the same expected for Regina. But, the young girl had been second to alcohol, gambling and men for such a time until the adjustment to her cousin was an easy one.

Regina still slept on the cot that had been purchased for her when she lived in the small apartment on 10th Street. Carla purchased a red mahogany high post bed with a firm, comfortable mattress and matching dresser for Elantra. It was imperative to assure her niece that she would not be treated second handed but she did so at the expense of her own child. Regina was told that Carla under no circumstances believed in junk food. Cold cereals (high in sugar) and fast food was provided for the Elantra so that she would feel at home and yet such foods were never allowed in the refrigerator prior to that time.

Elantra was so selfish. If Regina ate snacks that actually belonged to both of them, she would physically assault her for it. Carla's rescue attempts were unable to prevent the altercations from taking place. Again, Regina was reminded of the feelings of lack of protection that she had experienced with Daddy Jay. Everyone's well-being and feelings seemed to mean more to Carla but, the child's perception of the situation was incorrect. Regina was much too flexible and willing to compromise and therefore these qualities led to her needs inadvertently being ignored. It was always assumed that everything was all right with her when most often it was not. Her good attitude was a good excuse for her feelings to be disregarded.

CHAPTER 29

It had been years since Carla visited her hometown of Florence, South Carolina. Just before the Christmas season of 1974, Carla felt an overwhelming desire to go home. She contacted an aunt who remained stationary for all of the years Carla had been away. Elantra went to visit her older brother in Bridgeport for the holiday and Regina and Carla arrived in Florence the day before Christmas and remained through New Year's day.

Because of the slower pace of the little town, Regina was allowed more freedom and was less restricted in her play. It was liberating to play along the dirt roads with no regard for safety. Back in Philadelphia, Regina was instructed to only play on Warnock Street. She was not to venture out beyond the 2500 block for any reason without permission. And now she played with cousins that she had just met but was as comfortable as if she had spent a lifetime with them.

Carla met a man who made sure he gained her attention. He offered to drive her to visit any of her relatives she so desired to see, just to win her over. He offered her the moon and the stars and yet possessed very little to do so with but, his heart seemed to be in the right place and his appearance did not curtail the interest Carla developed for him. Omar McDonald was ten years Carla's senior. He was not very articulate and spoke with a heavy southern drawl. He was extremely dark complexioned, slender except for the large stomach which slightly overlapped his belt, his head was completely bald and it resembled an egg because of the shape of the top portion. He visited every day and he even took it upon himself to be her designated taxi to the train station when it became departure time for her return north.

In April, Omar contacted Carla in hopes that he would be allowed to share time with her while he visited his sister in Philadelphia.

"Carla, it's so good to see ya'. I can't think 'bout nothin' else but you since ya' left. How ya' been?" Omar was not much for conversation but he put forth tremendous efforts to communicate with Carla.

"I've been fine. I'm kind of tired of the big city though. Since I visited this Christmas, I long for the peace and the quiet of the rural roads. I never should have come here in the first place but, I just tried to make it home. Somehow, I now realize that I have not succeeded. I'm even considering moving back to Florence in the near future." Carla merely spoke aloud and yet gave Omar instant hope of a future with his new interest.

"When will ya' be coming back home?" Omar wanted to know in advance when he would see her again.

"I don't know. I don't have the money to be traveling back and forth so much. I haven't really decided if I will be back any time soon. I'll just have to wait and see what happens. I'm on a fixed income and money doesn't grow on trees." Again, Carla found herself talking more to herself than in response to Omar.

"Look, Carla. I'm not a rich man. I'm just a po' boy from the country. I don't have much but I'd give my last dime to see ya'. If ya' say yawl come again Christmas, I'll send for ya' and Shegina." Omar was never able to pronounce Regina's name properly.

"Christmas is a ways off. But, if by Thanksgiving you still want to send for us, we will act on it then. Does that sound fair?" Carla asked.

"I knows that I'll want to see ya'. I can't wait." Omar was already excited.

Omar phoned Carla once a week to see how things were and also to let her know his mind was still on their visit at Christmas. Carla welcomed the inter- ruptions because the fights between Elantra and Regina had gotten much more intense and were quite disturbing and disruptive. Regina's general nature was to endure whatever.... come what may. But with the frequency of fights, she felt the need to inform her mother of her true feelings. She could not hold it in any longer. It was time to stand up for herself even if no one else would.

"Mom, I need to talk to you about Elantra." Regina was insistent.

"What's wrong with you two now?"

"It's not fair that Elantra has been here all this time and things for her have gotten better and worse for me." Regina's tone of voice was very sad. "Everything Elantra wants, she gets. And because I don't complain about any- thing, I'm left to do without. I don't mind sharing with her but, she doesn't want to share with me and it is my home and you are my mother." Regina had com- manded Carla's attentions with her statement.

"What things have gotten worse for you? What do you mean?" she inquired.

"Like yesterday morning........ Elantra wanted pancakes for breakfast and I wanted cold cereal. You told me I had to eat pancakes because she was fixing them. That wasn't fair. Just because she wants pancakes doesn't mean that I want them too. But, I was made to eat them anyway. That's just not fair." Regina's example was still fresh in her mother's mind. Only one example was needed but Regina continued.

"I've wanted a real bed and dresser like the rest of my friends for a long time. But you never had the money before and when Elantra came, you bought her the bed and the dresser that I have been asking for. And she won't even share the dresser with me. My dresses are hung on a nail behind the bedroom door and my panties and leotards are kept in your room. I know you do these things so that she can feel welcome here but you make me feel like I'm not welcome."

Carla, stunned to the point of being non-responsive, knew every word the child had spoken was the absolute truth. She had not even stopped to think about the effects of Elantra on Regina nor had she thought of how her daughter's life would change because of her cousin.

"Regina, I am sorry. I had no idea you felt this way. You really did well by waiting this long to come to me and I am so sorry you haven't been happy. I just wanted to show Elantra love because no one else had since her mom was put away. She holds a lot of bitterness and I thought I could love all that away. It hasn't worked so far but, I didn't mean to make you unhappy in the process. I'll try to be more fair in the future. The next time she wants to make pancakes and you prefer cereal, each of you can have what you want."

The child was saddened by the conversation she demanded with her mother. But something very positive derived from it. She had never been shown any type of affection from her mother. She never was allowed to sit on her mother's lap and not even to hold hands. For the very first time, Carla reached out to Regina with extended arms and embraced her. It was obvious she had not realized the implications of her actions with her niece and she was truly apologetic. The hug was warm and sincere and felt similar to those of her friend, Jesus, to the affection starved youngster. But neither of them realized, Carla had actually changed.

CHAPTER 30

Carla and Regina returned to South Carolina due to the fact that Omar was a man of his word. Train fare for two was wired on Thanksgiving so arrangements for travel could be made early enough to allow for a Christmas visit. Again, Elantra traveled to her brother in Bridgeport as she had previously.

Carla visited her first husband's sister, Viola, whom she had always been close with when she resided in Florence and relied on the telephone to maintain their long distance relationship. Viola's sister, Sally, also came to visit Carla and seemed genuinely pleased to see her after such a long time. The entire holiday season was joyous and thoughts of relocation became more than a passing fancy to Carla now. Her soul yearned to be there again.

"Omar, thank you for showing me such a wonderful Christmas. I really hate for it to end," Carla admitted.

"Well, it don't have to end. Just move on back down here. We can get married and ya' can be at home again like ya' really want to." That was his best sales pitch for marriage.

"I'm more tired of the big city than I've ever been and I know when I go back it will seem even worse for me. I can't really think about marrying you because even though you've been really kind to me, I still know nothing about you. I can move home without our getting married and we can date." Carla refused to allow her desire to return to Florence to be the incentive used to enter into another marriage. She was insistent upon separation of the two.

"Why move here to spend the same money to live as ya' do in Philly. Move here. Marry me and yawl have less to worry 'bout. Let me take care of ya', Carla. You can do what you want to with ya' money." Omar was passionate about her.

"If I marry you, I will have less income to work with because my late husband's Social Security will no longer come to me. I will still receive his money for Regina but that's it." Carla gave every effort to make Omar understand.

"My money'll takes the place of his. So yawl be the same but then yawl have me to love ya'. I'll have ya' to come home to and get old with."

Carla returned home to discuss the possibilities with Elantra. She had just become accustomed to Philly enough to say she had partially adjusted. She could not fathom or even entertain the thought of moving to South Carolina, though.

"Aunt Carla, I don't want to move to Florence with you. I'm not going. I want to go and live with my brother in Bridgeport. That's where I belong anyway." There was no cooperation from Elantra.

"I can't stay here any longer, Elantra. I never belonged here in the first place and it will never feel like home to me. I have a responsibility to you when I came and brought you here to live but, I can't sacrifice myself and my needs to do it." Carla fought desperately to make her niece see things from her perspective.

"I really appreciate what you have tried to do for me. What you haven't done already won't happen anyway. I know it hasn't been easy to bring me into your home and have another person to take care of. Even if you stay here, I don't belong here with you and it's never going to work. I want to go home to Connecticut and I want to live with my brother, Junior. I'm only going to be miserable and make everyone around me miserable until I can be where I want to be. I will only get worse in South Carolina because I would want to be there even less than here."

"OK. You've made your point. But, just remember, you have an aunt who truly cares about you and what happens to you. Don't ever think no one cared. I cared. I do understand though. I know about feeling like you are out of place and no matter what you do, the place still feels the same. Call your brother and we will see how he feels about taking care of you." Carla was very familiar with such feelings. She resided in Philadelphia for over 30 years and still was uncomfortable. Therefore, she was able to empathize.

Junior agreed that Elantra could live with him until she had finished school. Carla decided Omar's love for her was guarantee enough to agree to marry him. Regina greatly anticipated a calmer lifestyle than the city had offered her. And all was settled for the move to Florence and the separation of Elantra, Carla and Regina. Arrangements were made when the school term ended, Elantra would be transferred along with her things to Bridgeport. Carla, Regina and there belongings would be shipped via North American Van Lines south bound. Elantra was picked up the day before the movers were due to pack the furniture. And when the truck arrived, the driver insisted upon Carla and Regina accompanying him for the free ride to Florence on the truck verses spending the $105.00 by train. Regina watched the city skyline disappear slowly behind her and anxiously fantasized about her new life.

CHAPTER 31

Carla's arrival was the first experience inside of Omar's house even though he had driven her past it on one of their joy rides. It was an old wood framed white house trimmed in pale green that Omar built with his own hands for his first wife twenty years prior. There was a mile long dirt road which extended from Bannockburn Road (the main paved street). The dirt road forked one half mile past Omar and continued for three miles where his son, G.E. and his daughter, Eliza lived. On one side of the house, there was the kitchen, den and living room. And on the other, there were two bedrooms and a bath. The five room dwelling had only one source of heat which was a kerosene fueled heater centrally located in the room used as a small den between the kitchen and the living room. Air conditioning was considered a unneeded luxury which explained why it was nonexistent. There was a crack in the living room ceiling large enough to view the starlit sky at night and the sunny blue sky of a clear day. Carla repainted every room with bright colors to add life to them and to give it her own personal touch. She bought frilly curtains for both the kitchen and the bathroom to mask the masculine feel.

Omar was extremely old fashioned and set in his ways. He expected his converted city wife and her northern daughter to automatically adjust to the somewhat primitive ways he had adapted to all his life. He insisted on raising chickens, pigs and there was even a vegetable garden which provided food for the animals and the family. Carla was now responsible for the upkeep of it all. Off to the right, if facing the house, was a barn where the farm tools and food harvested from the small farm were kept. It was not the lifestyle either of the two females would have chosen for themselves but, Carla was positive and willing to make the best home possible with plans that more suitable housing would soon follow. Omar, was satisfied with the current living arrangements and had no intentions of change. Sharing his life with two other people was all the contribution he desired to make.

Regina enjoyed the long rides on her bicycle without supervision. She was the only girl among Omar's four grandsons who quickly accepted their new aunt

as a desirable playmate. They did everything together; from building club hous-
es in the woods, swinging in the tire in the tree in the front yard, to playing softball in a near-by field. For the first time, it was no longer necessary for her to run
to and from school to avoid the attacks of white gangs who tormented the gifted
black children bussed to the Magnet program in their neighborhood. There were
no more seven block trips to school in ten inches of snow during the winter and
the weather was much more mild than what she was accustomed to. Everything
changed. Now, there was a school bus which picked her up at the front door and
dropped her off at the end of the day. But, had everything really changed?

Carla sat on the porch to catch the breeze of the day. Dinner was prepared.
The house was neat and tidy as always. Regina arrived from school which had
just begun its session two weeks earlier.

"Hi, Mom," Regina greeted Carla as she headed inside to put down her book
bag and to grab a snack.

"Hello. I've been waiting for you because I know you don't have a key to
the house and I wanted to walk back to Eliza's just to get out for a while," Carla
said.

"OK, I'm going to fix me a peanut butter and jelly sandwich and milk. I'll
do my homework and then I will feed the chickens like Daddy said."

"I should be back before he gets home but if not, dinner is already on the
stove." Carla walked down the dirt road for her visit with Eliza.

While she talked with Omar's daughter, she learned of how mean, evil and
miserly he had been during his first marriage until his wife's death. It came as
such a surprise to Carla because she had not experienced that side of him yet and
actually found him to be quite generous up until that point. She listened but
somehow convinced herself that she was exempt from such behaviors. Upon her
arrival back home she saw the beginning of his true ways as they revealed themselves slowly but surely. Omar's car was parked by the back door as he did daily
when he returned home from work. Carla found Regina in the den with her
homework and books but it was noticeable that she had been crying. Omar was
on the front porch and had not yet eaten.

"Regina, what's the matter?" Carla questioned.

"I got a spanking," Regina gave her short but direct response.

Carla frowned and looked into her child's face with much concern. "What
did you get a spanking for? What did you do?"

"Daddy said I had to feed the chickens when I got home from school. Every
day I've been feeding them first, then getting myself a snack and homework. I
was really hungry today because I didn't like what they had on the menu for
lunch and I didn't want to waste my lunch money if I wasn't going to eat the
food. So, I decided to wait until I got home to eat. Daddy came home and I had-
n't shelled the corn so I could feed the chickens and he told me I didn't do what
he told me, and then he spanked me and sent me out to do the chores. I tried to
explain that I was going to feed them but, I was really hungry and wanted to eat

something first. But, he wouldn't listen. He told me never feed myself before I feed his chickens. He said that I was to feed them as soon as I get off the school bus. My hands hurt so bad already from shelling corn barehanded and the blisters have already burst open. I'm not used to this kind of work. I don't mind doing my share but, I think he's being unfair," Regina cried as she relived her last conversation with Omar.

Carla walked onto the porch to ask her husband his version of what happened. "Omar, why haven't you eaten. The food is cooked and ready." Carla's curiosity was peaked as she noticed no dishes in the sink as evidence that he had eaten.

"I didn't eat because my food wasn't ready when I got home," he snapped.

"That's not true. I cooked chicken and dumplings, cornbread and black-eyed peas. They are sitting on the stove, Omar."

"My food ain't ready 'less it's hot and sittin' on a plate fo' me to eat. That's what I got a wife fo'."

"OK. I'll heat up the food and fix your plate but, what's wrong with Regina?" she inquired of him as though she had not yet spoken to her daughter.

"She just mad 'cause I told ha' to feed them chickens like I told ha' to and I popped ha' fo' times on the butt 'cause she ain't listenin' to me."

"She's never done these things before Omar, she didn't realize there was a certain time they needed to be fed by. Did you take the time to explain it to her? Couldn't you have talked to her about it this time and then if she still didn't do as you asked then you could say she was being disobedient and spank her?"

Regina could hear them going back and forth with the argument and she hated the fact she was the topic of conversation. She wanted and needed their attention but under no circumstances did she want such negative exposure. She resolved within herself just to do whatever he asked, however he asked so as to keep the peace. But, she was not the source of the tension in the house.

Carla was also given nearly impossible tasks to complete. Omar allotted $25.00 per week for groceries and no more. The amount was not just for food but for cleaning supplies and snacks as well. Through the couple's bickering and arguing, Regina also learned her mother was paying $10.00 per month on the electric bill so the child could watch television. Omar felt the 13" black and white TV Regina watched in the den, burned too much electricity and he wanted to be compensated for that usage. Once the winter set in, Omar would turn off the heater at his bedtime of 8:00 p.m. because he believed the covers trapped enough body heat to keep from burning the heater all night. Regina and Carla would drink less toward nightfall so their bladders would not demand that they leave their beds until morning.

Carla compromised time and time again but, there was no such thing with Omar. He was sure to make it known that little if anything would change in his life. Even though his home now belonged to two others, it was his way or no way and there was never any room for him to give in.

CHAPTER 32

C arla spent an enormous amount of time alone in the house. To not drive in Florence was much more of a hindrance than in Philadelphia because public transportation in the small town was so very limited. It was pointless to put forth the time and the effort just to go a few short blocks. Whenever there was an argument between Omar and Carla, he hurried to his automobile and escaped the ill feelings that were present. Day after day, Carla felt more trapped. She could only gain new surroundings when she was driven and most of the neighbors were so busied with their own lives until it was more of a comfort to wait for Omar to return. At the age of 52, Carla was determined to learn to drive but, Omar knew if she was to become independent, she would be less dependent on him. He needed her to remain reliant upon him and so he always provided an excuse not to teach her. However, there was a silver lining to her marital cloud. The time she spent alone with Regina actually served as a good experience because it promoted her to conversations which built their relationship as mother and daughter.

"I am so tired of sitting here alone all the time. When you are out playing, it gets so lonely for me. Yes, I read my Bible which has been real helpful to me to endure this life but, I want to be able to go to the store without having to wait to see if Omar feels like taking me. I'd like to visit some of my friends after church on some Sundays. I feel so trapped most of the time. You are too young to really understand any of this but, you are the only person I can talk to." Carla was expecting no real response because she was talking aloud to herself.

"Mom, you can use my money from Daddy Jay to get somebody to teach you how to drive. The high school has a driving class and maybe there are some driving schools for adults. If you want to learn to drive then try to find some numbers from the phone book and see how much it costs. It won't hurt to try." Regina rationalized more successfully than most adults and even more than Carla imagined. Her response made a lot of sense and even though her mother actually did not need her daughter's permission to utilize the Social Security check from Jay, it was comforting to know that her child was in agreement for whatever the use.

Carla's cousin, Johnny and his wife Dorene, lived a half mile up on Bannockburn Road. Dorene was quite fond of Carla yet not equally so for Omar. Carla first received a driver's handbook from her cousin-in-law and studied it. Then Dorene took her to get her learner's permit. And for the last portion of her plan, Carla found Taggart Driving School which was the most reasonable and provided both pick up and drop off as often as she desired. Their prices were based upon each lesson and much more affordable for the schedule that Carla required. Taggart was instructed to pick her up at 9:00 a.m. on Monday, Wednesday and Friday of each week, Omar would be at work and he would not be made aware of her outside endeavors. The school taught Carla the proper driving terminology and techniques which she learned very quickly.

One Wednesday morning, Omar decided that his daily agenda would not include work because he felt ill. Carla was not presented with the opportunity to call for cancellation of the scheduled driving lesson. After pondering the dilemma, she decided it really did not matter whether her husband learned of her lessons or not, especially because the burden of payment was not his responsibility. When the yellow car pulled up to the house with black letters which spelled *"Taggart"*, Omar was totally taken by surprise. He had no knowledge of what the words on the car read because he had no more than a third grade education. But, Carla was ready and left no room for his questions by rushing to enter the driver's side of the car. He was at a loss for words as he watched her, in astonishment, pull away and signal left to approach the dirt road. To Carla's surprise, he did not mention the lessons or the availability of those funds when she returned.

In two month's time, Carla had obtained her learner's permit, professional driving instructions and was ready to take the driving test. Dorene provided the car for testing because Omar had flatly refused. Carla did exceptionally well and was successful with her very first attempt. She then saved the $300.00 a month of Regina's money to save for a car of her own because she was not foolish enough to believe Omar was ever going to willingly share his vehicle having never done so before. His first wife did not drive. Carla was inclined to do without the hassle of having to ask and then being rejected. So, after three months, Dorene took Carla to purchase her first car, a 1969 Dodge Dart. Omar added Carla's car onto his insurance and it allowed him to be eligible for a considerable second vehicle discount. There had to be a motive and benefit for him.

Food prices rose and yet Carla was not given any additional money. Consequently, there was less groceries brought into the house and more reason to accept Omar's complaints. He failed to see that prices had risen.

"Hell, ya' keep sayin' food's gone up. But, ya' can buy drivin' lessons, a car and insurance. Why ya' can't help with food?" Omar actually felt cheated.

"You were the one who told me I could do whatever I wanted with Regina's check. You were the one who said you wanted to take care of me. Well, damn it, do it! Take care of me! I do help with food, Omar. I buy snacks that I am not able to buy with the measly $25.00 per week grocery money you give me for three people. I also buy soap and dish washing liquid and all my personal items. I purchase gas for your car when you take me someplace where you had not planned to go. Yes, I had to get lessons, a car and was prepared to pay insurance because you wouldn't do it for me. You were not even willing to share your car or time to teach me how to drive. If you had, I wouldn't have had to go out and do it on my own!"

"Ya' didn't hafta' learn to drive. I take ya' wherever ya' want to go!" He actually believed what he had just stated.

"How do you even know where I want to go when you go to work all day, and come home to eat and off you go again. You wouldn't know because as long as I'm providing your needs, mine don't matter to you. I'm only as good as the meals I prepare and the sex I provide. But, I have needs too! You haven't taken the time to find out if I have plans outside of going to the grocery store or paying a bill. I wanted a car so I could go where I wanted to go; not just where it was absolutely necessary. There is a big difference!" Carla shouted.

"Just 'cause ya' got a car don't mean ya' can go where ya' want to no way. Ya' still can't go 'til I tell ya' to." Omar's intentions were to remain in control.

"You have lost your mind if you think I'm going to call your job and ask your permission to drive up to Dorene's or go to the mall to window shop. There is nothing under God's green earth that says I have to do that!" Carla used a threatening tone of voice.

"Carla, ya' and that gal can get the hell out of my house if ya' can't do what I say!" Omar was furious.

"I asked you to never say that to me again. This is the third time you've told me to get out of your house. It is obvious this will never be my home and you will never allow it to be. You don't like my daughter and you make it painfully clear daily. I didn't come down here to live in a spider infested, hole in the wall for you to make me and my daughter's life miserable. You beat on her for the simplest things and make her do the chores that you yourself hate to do as a man. I told you the last time you told me to get out of your house, that if you told me once more I would give you your wish. You won't buy enough food for us. We freeze like crazy in the winter because you are too cheap to provide fuel for the heater. I caught pneumonia this winter and you still said, "Yawl, it ain't cold in here." My child can't even watch TV without me having to pay you for the extra watts it uses. Omar, you are full of shit! I am trying to be a good wife to you and you have no idea how much I have changed. But, I'm no longer going to allow you to mistreat my daughter and misuse and abuse me. You'll pay for telling me to get out. Do you hear me? You will pay!" Carla had plans in mind.

111

CHAPTER 33

It was now May and Omar's last threat for Carla to vacate took place in January. Because there was no mention of it again by either, it was assumed all was forgiven and forgotten. But, Carla rarely made a threat she had no intention of keeping and all she needed was time to bring her business in order and a way to put her plan into action. Nothing changed for her and with each passing day, the echo of Omar's verbal eviction haunted her. She felt as though she was an absolute fool for her continued unwelcome stay. And sleep escaped her most nights while she occupied herself by looking over at her husband as she plotted her way out of the marriage.

Regina noticed two girls who stayed on the school bus past her stop. She often wondered where they lived and if it was close enough for her to visit. She dared not invite anyone to her house often because everyone who knew of her stepfather, feared him. One day, she rode her bicycle 1/2 mile past Eliza's house and found she was no longer limited to playing with boys. The Ellis family had a son and adjacent to the right of them was the Bacon family whom the two girls from the school bus belonged. Melanie was the youngest and Dorothy was the eldest of the two. Regina never met a stranger and so she boldly walked up to the side door underneath the carport and knocked on the door. Melanie came to view and recognized her bus mate immediately.

"Hi, I'm Regina. I ride the same bus as you. What's your name?"

"Melanie," the fair complexioned young girl replied with a smile.

"Can you come outside and play?"

"Let me ask my mother." She turned to face Dawn, who stood a few feet away in the kitchen.

Dawn looked out through the screened door to get a glimpse of the new child in the neighborhood to find her smiling back at her.

"Hello, I'm Regina. Can Melanie come outside and play with me?" This time she directed her question to Dawn and the adult found that to be most pleasing.

"Yes, she can go out but, I want her to stay in the yard," Dawn advised.

Regina could hardly wait to start her new friendship. "How old are you, Melanie?"

"I'm 10. I'll be 11 on my birthday this month. How old are you?" Melanie wanted to get as much information as she could.

"I just turned 13," Regina responded.

Day after day Regina would come to visit the Bacon family. She told her mother about how much fun she had and how nice the girls were. Dorothy was beautiful and had the loveliest dark complexioned skin Regina had ever seen. She was very quiet-natured yet, Regina found her to be extremely pleasant. She seemed to just enjoy watching everyone else participate in conversations and games of softball. She was 15 and would turn 16 on her next birthday in July. There was also an older sibling, Tina.

Mr. Bacon was employed away from the home and Mrs. Bacon's full-time job was to attend to the house and run the medium-sized family farm. It consisted of pigs, chickens, gardens of peas, tomatoes, cabbage and they had a large crop of tobacco with a curing barn in which to dry it for sale. The family worked exceptionally hard but was equally as happy and content with their lifestyle. Regina found herself wondering what made life so wonderful for some and so tragic for those like herself. When the time came for the Bacon family's focus to shift to the tobacco crop, their cousin Roland Ellis always worked with them to earn money for school clothes the next year. He was the same age as Melanie. Regina knew nothing about working in the tobacco fields but she did not desire segregation from her friends. If it was necessary for them to work, then she would do the same, with Mrs. Bacon's permission.

"Ms. Dawn, I learn really fast and I can do anything I put my mind to. Yes, I'm from the city and a lot of things people do down south, I haven't done. But, I want to learn and I want to help you so that I can still spend time with Melanie and Dorothy. I won't be in the way, I promise. I'll learn what you teach me and I'll be good and fast at it. Can I please work with you?" Regina was sincere and adamant. Dawn could clearly see this and therefore, with no hesitation took the child up on her offer.

"Yes, you can work with us. But, you have to ask your mother if it is all right because we work from 6:30 in the morning until sunset on most days. You don't have to worry about lunch and I will pay you by the day for helping us. Dorothy, give Regina the telephone number and have her mother to call me to let me know if it is OK."

Regina was excited because she would experience some things that she had never even imagined before she came to South Carolina. She was so very fond of Dorothy and Melanie until the idea of working hard meant nothing compared to the idea of not being able to spend time with them.

"Mom, I really want to work with them. I can do it! If Melanie and Dorothy can do it, I know that I can learn and it won't take me long," she encouraged.

"Regina, you spend an awful lot of time with these people. They don't need you around interrupting their work. Leave them alone so they can do their farming in peace." Carla had not yet noticed the excitement in Regina because of her preoccupation with plans to leave Omar.

"They said they could use the help and Mrs. Bacon said she would teach me everything there is to learn. You know I learn fast and I know I can do it. Melanie and Dorothy's cousin, Roland, helps them every year and she's even going to pay me. She says for you to call her if you have questions or if you agree to let me work with them." She handed the piece of paper with the telephone number written on it and urged her to pick up the phone. Carla dialed the number that her daughter anxiously shoved in her direction.

"Hello, may I speak to Mrs. Dawn Bacon, please?"

"I'm Dawn," Mrs. Bacon answered.

"This is Regina's mother, Carla. How are you?"

"I'm fine, thank you."

"Regina is very excited about working with you in your tobacco fields. She told me to call you to let you know that she has my permission."

"Mrs. Carla, I will be responsible for your daughter. She will not leave my sight and I will give her lunch. Did she tell you I will pay her $30.00 per day?"

"No, she didn't mention the amount of money which lets me know she cares more about spending time with your girls than she has interest in money. I'm really glad she thinks so much of them because she's not had too many lasting friendships. We've moved around quite a bit. If it means that much to her and you will see to her safety, I can't say no. You seem like such a nice person and I would like to come and meet you just so that I know who my child will be spending all her time with. She has spoken highly of you and I would like to get to know you myself." Carla hadn't realized since she exchanged her lifestyle of drinking and gambling for Christianity, she was much more the mother that Regina always longed for.

"I look forward to meeting you. But, it will have to be before Monday because that's when I'll start in the tobacco field. Why don't you come by today?" Dawn found Carla pleasant and looked forward to meeting her face to face. She also wondered about the woman Omar McDonald had married. She surmised about a woman who could marry a man with such a mean reputation.

"I have a few things to finish up here at home. But, I will come back there around 3:30. How does that sound to you?"

"That time is good for me. I'll see you then." Dawn hung up the phone.

Carla drove the cream Dodge with the black interior and black vinyl top down the road past Eliza's, the Ellis' and started her right turn into the Bacon's yard. On both sides of the entire dirt road were huge ditches. If the vehicle was not maneuvered with expert precision, it was easy to misjudge and get entangled in the ditch banks. Carla's inexperience caused her to land the left front wheel of the car in the ditch. Dawn looked out of the door just as it occurred.

"Carla, are you all right?"

114

"Yes," she answered. "I thought I cleared that ditch, though." Carla slid across the front seat to get out on the opposite side and the car slipped further in the ditch.

"Stay where you are. I'll get the tractor and pull you out." Dawn was accustomed to these happenings and knew exactly what to do. She took a large chain and attached one end to the back of the tractor and the other to the back of the car. She instructed Carla to turn the steering wheel so the tread of the tire rested straight against the bank of the ditch and the Dodge was immediately freed from the dirt prison.

"What a welcome mat that was," Dawn joked.

"Yes, it scared me. But, at least there was very little damage done to the car. I'll learn to be better at judging my distance next time. Thank you so much for getting me out."

"Oh, no problem. I was glad to help. I have ended up in that ditch a time or two myself. That's how I knew how to get you out so easily. Don't feel bad. It happened to quite a few people." Dawn did her best to assure Carla that her driving ability was not in question.

The two women talked until 5:00 p.m. and the only reason for the cease was Carla's need to return home in order to have Omar's meal prepared on a plate upon his arrival. Carla gave her consent for Regina to work with Dawn and they both vowed to get together soon just for a friendly chat. Little did they know, at the time, that their new friendship would blossom into a support system that both women needed so desperately.

CHAPTER 34

Regina began her work with the Bacon's as planned the following Monday after Carla met with Dawn at her home. All went well and even though the work was exhausting and the heat was extreme, the converted city girl embraced the openness of the outdoors and the fresh country air. The crops grew tall and there were endless rows to hoe to excavate the weeds from around the tobacco plants. There must have been at least two acres or more and Omar's grandchildren helped if only to suffice their desire to be near Regina, Melanie and Dorothy. Three weeks went by and there was a brief break before more work was to be completed. Carla arranged her move for Monday. She traveled down the long dirt road to visit her newly found friend and to gain assistance with her plans to vacate Omar's premises.

"Hello, Dawn. How are things with you today?" She located Dawn out by the pen where the pigs were kept. She had progressed more than midway the feeding process.

"Oh, great. I'm just looking after my hogs. There is always something that needs to be done when you run a farm no matter how large or small it is," Dawn said as she continued to work.

"I didn't come to interrupt you. I just wanted to talk." Carla knew the importance of Dawn's farm and was very careful not to intrude. She was amazed by the amount her friend was able to accomplish and she handled every aspect of the farm like an extreme professional. Dorothy immediately presented herself outside to assist her mother.

"I'll be finished in just a minute. I don't have very much left to do at all and I would like to sit and talk with you. Go inside and get something cool to drink and rest until I come in. We can talk then." Dawn urged Carla away from the sun exposure having noticed the large beads of perspiration on her forehead.

Carla went inside and Melanie gave her a large glass of cool water. Tina was sitting in the den and Carla was instructed to take a chair opposite the television set so that it may serve as entertainment for her until Dawn came inside. Within 15 minutes, Dawn stood on the back porch of the large brick house and removed her coverall jumpsuit and shoes then entered from the back entrance directly into the den where Carla sat.

"Dorothy, please get me something cool to drink?" she asked as she sat down on the sofa across from Carla.

"Are you finished for the day?" Carla could not imagine having to do more than what she had already witnessed.

"Yeah, there's nothing more I can do. But, I'll start bright and early tomorrow with a whole new list of things. So, what's on your mind? You seemed to have been in deep thought when I first came in." Dawn had noticed Carla's distant stare in the direction of the television.

"Well, I really can't deal with Omar and his evil ways anymore. He told me several months ago to get out of his house and at the time I didn't have money or plans. That was not the first time he told me to get out and I promised him the next time he said it to me would be his last. He hasn't said it since but, I have taken all I am going to from him. I've contacted my sister-in-law, Viola, and she says Regina and I can stay with her until I am able to find a place of my own. I could have moved out a couple of months ago but, I want to get divorced before I leave or at least have it started so my second husband's Social Security will be returned to me. With that money and the amount we receive for Regina, it will be enough to survive with. But everything has to be done in order. I can't afford to make any mistakes. I will be moving my belongings into storage on Monday and I want to know if Dorothy can help me and Regina pack? We can't begin until he leaves for work and we must have everything gone before he comes home."

"It's fine with me if she wants to help you. There's not anything I have planned for her on Monday but, you'll need to ask her. Carla you seem like such a nice woman and I hate things didn't work out with your marriage. I will pray everything turns out the way you want it to. No one deserves to be mistreated and I couldn't advise anyone to allow someone to treat them bad. My husband is good to me and he has provided all of my needs and the majority of my wants. I couldn't ask for a better man than Jackson but, I can't tell you how I would feel if he treated me the way you've described. I can't say you're right or wrong for leaving but, I don't think anyone should have to live in that kind of misery. I'm not here to judge you or to tell you what to do. Do what you feel is right for you and only God knows what that is," Dawn explained.

Carla looked over at Dorothy who was standing in the doorway of the kitchen and the den. "Would you help us pack our things on Monday? I will give you something for your time."

"I don't mind. I'll help you move," Dorothy quickly responded.

"Omar leaves for work at 7:00 a.m. and I would like to start the minute he disappears from sight. I will call you when he's gone and if you could be ready, it would help me." Carla seemed relieved that the last piece to the puzzle was now in place. Monday's arrival was all that was needed and all the pieces would come together.

"Mom, I like Auntie Viola but, there are no kids for me to play with there. Can I stay here with Mrs. Dawn for the rest of the Summer so I can keep working with her?" Regina resisted her entire world being changed.

Carla glimpsed in Dawn's direction to view her reaction to the child's question. She noticed a warm smile which could only have meant that she was pleased that Regina found working with her favorable.

"I will have to talk with Jackson tonight when he gets home to see how he feels about it. Regina works hard and she isn't a bit of trouble, is a big help and is pleasant to have around. I would love to have her and I know Dorothy and Melanie are quite fond of her too. I'll talk it over with Jackson and call you tonight," Dawn said.

"Well, I'd better get back before Omar gets home. I don't want to give him a single sign that anything is wrong. Plus, I want to make sure I get past the ditch again and I can see better while it is still daylight. Dawn, thank you for everything. Your support means a lot and I am grateful to you. Please tell Jackson I will pay for her staying here if he decides to let her continue to work."

"You will not have to pay us anything. I know Jackson will feel the same. He is quite attached to Regina and he knows how good of a worker she is. All we need to do is to check with him and I know that he will agree. Like I said, I will call you tonight as soon as I get the OK. Just relax about it," Dawn persuaded.

Carla returned home in time to prepare Omar's plate and his drink sat cooled on the table.

CHAPTER 35

M onday finally became a reality and Carla cooked sausage, eggs and grits for breakfast which was the usual morning ritual. She sent Omar off to work with a bologna and cheese sandwich for lunch by 7:00 a.m. and as soon as his car could no longer be seen over the hill, she made the call for Dorothy's assistance.

"Good morning, Dawn. How are you doing?" Carla asked.

"I'm fine. Did you want me to send Dorothy to help you now?" Dawn remembered that time was of the essence.

"Yes, Regina is walking that way now to meet her. And thank you again for letting her help," Carla stated with much gratitude.

Ten minutes after the conversation with Dawn, Dorothy and Regina arrived on the front porch. The boxes that were to be used for the move were inside a U-haul truck behind the house of her cousin, located on Bannonckburn Road.

"Girls, the first thing you can do is to pull all of the dishes out of the cabinets and place them on the table so they can be wrapped with newspaper and packed." Carla pulled three large stacks of newspaper she had hidden under the sofa in the den and piled them onto the table.

"I will be back in a minute with the truck and the boxes. When you finish that, just start to pull the pictures off the walls that belong to me and be careful not to remove any nails, you might take down an entire wall by mistake," she teased. "Oh, take down the curtains in the kitchen and the bathroom only."

Carla returned with the truck and boxes and the girls worked feverishly and yet carefully to get everything inside. By 12:00 p.m. the last of her belongings were loaded and Carla, Regina and Dorothy cleaned each room immaculately before the keys to the house were placed on the kitchen counter adjacent to the sink and the doors to each entrance were locked for the final time. From the outside, there was no evidence to suspect the change that had taken place until entry. At 2:20, Carla and the girls unloaded the last box into the storage space on Irby Street that would house the furnishings and household goods until Carla had a residence to call her own. Dorene followed close behind for the truck return and provided transportation back to Dawn's.

"Dorothy, you were such a big help to me today. I could never have done everything without you. Here's $20.00 for your hard work. It's not much in comparison to what you did for me but it's all I can spare right now. I will give you a little something when I get it," Carla explained.

"No, Ms. Carla. I didn't mind helping you. You don't have to give me anything. I wanted to help," and she gently pushed Carla's hand which held the twenty dollar bill away from her.

"You worked hard. I want you to have it."

"I wanted to do it. I don't want any money," Dorothy said respectfully.

"Well, you are a good friend to Regina and I really appreciate you." Carla gave a warm and caring smile.

At 5:20, Dorene called Carla at Viola's. "Carla, Omar is so upset. His daughter, Eliza, said he walked up and down the dirt road three times already since he got home. He came to her for answers because he was sure you could not have moved out and not told anyone."

"The last person I would tell would be his daughter if I didn't want him to know about it. She can't hold water. She talks too much. I really don't want to talk about Omar right now, though. I just got away from there and he needs time to talk to God about the things he caused to happen. Thanks for letting me know but, all I want to do is get a hot bath and go to bed. I'll talk to you later, OK?"

"I'm sure it's been a hard day for you. Get some rest." Dorene ended the call. Two minutes passed and Omar appeared in her driveway. She refused to be placed in the middle but, she did sympathize and so she listened.

"Dorene, is Carla here with you?" Omar appeared physically ill.

"No, she's not. Come in and have a seat." His facial expression instantly made her aware of his need to talk.

"Ha' left me. Ha' took ha' stuff and the gal and they gone. Do ya' know where they at?"

"Slow down Omar. Tell me what happened. Tell me why you think she left." Dorene evaded the question so as not to lie and she was equally determined not to betray Carla's trust.

"I got home, opened the door and all ha' stuff was gone. Ha' left all the stuff I had but ......," he abruptly halted and broke down in tears.

CHAPTER 36

C arla continued to live with Viola as the end of the summer neared. Regina valued her friends and the time they shared but, she missed her mother terribly. She utilized the telephone number given to her when Carla first separated from Omar once a week and she only used it to say hello and for small talk. But that Tuesday she called to gain information; answers to questions only Carla was able to supply.

"Hi Mommy, how is Aunt Vi doing?" Regina always showed such concern for others.

"She's doing fine. She asked about you the other day and I told her I hadn't talked to you this week."

"Well, Dorothy and Melanie are getting ready for school and I wanted to know where I'm going. Have you found us a place to live yet?"

"There are three more weeks before school actually begins, Regina. I have to go and check on some apartments where Aunt Sally used to live and she's going to talk to the manager to make sure we get in. I just hope they have an apartment vacant. I'm going to come and get you on Friday, so make sure you have all your things packed and we will go and get school clothes after we check on the apartment. Did you enjoy your time with the Bacons?" Carla recognized the absence of frequent calls as a sure indication that she had but just wanted to hear it from her daughter.

"Oh, yes! We had fun and Ms. Dawn was so nice to me. She treated me just like Dorothy and Melanie. But, I missed you." There was a sadness to Regina's tone.

"I know you did. I missed you too. Let me speak to Dawn before I go. And remember to make sure you pack all of your things and be ready when I come to pick you up on Friday," Carla instructed.

"OK, here's Ms. Dawn," she said as she handed the receiver to the lady of the house.

"Hello."

"Hello, Dawn. How are things today?"

"Oh, I have no complaints. How are you?"

"I'm still trying to get things together as far as living arrangements but, I have to admit things are not nearly as grim as I imagined they would be. I was able to get my Social Security returned to me and I received my first check last week. By the way, I will be coming to pick Regina up on Friday afternoon and I really want to thank you for taking such good care of her for me. She cares for you and she told me you treat her just like your own. That means more to me than I can say and maybe one day I will be able to repay you for what you've done for us. How much do I owe you?" Carla was truly grateful and would have generously compensated whatever Dawn requested.

"Regina was no trouble to me at all. It was easy to treat her as my own because she obeyed me and behaved with such manners. She is a good girl and the pleasure was all mine. She worked for her stay here. She worked hard, she learned quickly and was a big help from the very start. I couldn't charge you anything as I told you before. She earned her keep," Dawn smiled as she reflected over the past six weeks.

"Well, may God bless you because you did a much needed favor for me. I will never forget it. Thank You."

"You're very welcome, Carla. I'll see you on Friday at about 4:30."

"Yes. Take care," Carla replied.

Carla returned to the Bacon home promptly at 4:30 to retrieve her daughter. Just as she had instructed, Regina had all of her things packed neatly in her suitcase which sat under the carport. She hugged Dorothy first because the two had grown extremely close and there was a special bond between them. She then, hugged Melanie, Tina, Dawn, Roland and Omar's three grandsons who came to say good-bye as well. She waved as Carla maneuvered the Dodge Dart with much more confidence and ease than previous times, and sped down the dirt road to leave nothing but a trail of dust in the air.

Regina was excited about the prospective new apartment and Carla took her to view it. Oakland Heights was located in North Florence on Oakland Avenue and was very well kept. The most appealing thing for Carla was that rent was based upon income. She was hopeful that she would be able to make a fairly decent life for herself and her daughter and prayed for an availability. When they returned on Monday, the only vacancy was a three bedroom townhouse. The expense would decrease for a two bedroom which was perceived as the perfect size for them but, Carla's desperation for independence caused the acceptance of the three bedroom in spite of the additional charge. However, she was given the transfer option as soon as a smaller unit became available. She insisted the three bedroom was meant for them. She paid the deposit and the first month's rent, the manager gave her the keys and the three of them inspected the apartment.

It was beautiful and spacious. The walls were freshly painted white and the floors and every aspect of the grounds were so clean and fresh. Once inside, Carla realized the three bedroom was going to hold her furniture and the two bedroom definitely would not have accommodated all her household goods. There was an additional entrance to the back of the apartment which faced Oakland Avenue and because the townhouse was located on the corner, windows cast an abundance of light throughout the entire dwelling. The first floor consisted of a living room, dining room, kitchen, 1/2 bath and storage area. On the second level, there were three large bedrooms and a full bath.

It was the first of the month and the rent on the storage space was due. Living quarters was obtained just in time to save another month's rental fee. Things progressed much more quickly than Carla anticipated and she stopped periodically to catch her breath so that she could regroup. She once again recruited Dorothy's help and the girl's teamwork made the removal of the boxes from the rental space to the apartment a breeze. It seemed to Carla that Dorothy and Regina moved together daily because the comparison between the two moves was like night and day. Everything flowed with such ease. Carla hired two of Viola's neighbors and they transported the bedroom furniture to the upper level. Carla was confident in the girl's ability to get the rest of the job done as she returned the men home now that each piece of furniture was in its appropriate room and retrieved her belongings from Viola's. She made calls from there to have the electricity changed over into her name and phone services established.

Regina found she had a talent for arranging furniture and created such a warm decor. She instructed Dorothy as to where pictures were to be hung and the placement of floor rugs. When Carla returned home she was so pleasantly surprised by their accomplishments and even though there were still boxes to be unpacked, all the furnishings were in place including lamps on the end tables. So, Carla treated her eager helpers to McDonald's and returned Dorothy home. Yes, Regina regretted the repeated separations from her friend yet, she was eager to return home. She wanted to put everything in its proper place and assess the apartment in its most completed state. She worked all the rest of the evening and into the early morning until all was finished. There was no furniture for Regina's room, but determination to sleep there seduced her as she gathered several quilts, a blanket and a pillow and made herself comfortable on the floor where she pleasantly visited sleep for several hours that morning.

CHAPTER 37

The apartment on Oakland Avenue served as a exceptionally happy home for Regina and Carla. The neighbors in the three adjacent apartments were all delightful people and each planned to maintain residence there indefinitely.

All was well with school also. Regina was informed of a bus which traveled from Oakland Heights to Southside Jr. High School everyday and allowed her to remain with the friends she had gained while living with Omar. The bus driver was a handsome, fair complexioned young man with freckles, who was in his senior year at South Florence High, located directly beside the Jr. High. And Regina immediately developed a school-girl crush. She anxiously awaited the long drive to and from school daily just to be near him yet, he was cordial, quiet and never gave a clue that he remotely noticed her beyond being a passenger on his bus. Her feelings of devotion to him prompted the decision to remain on board even though there was an opportunity to exit three miles prior to the last stop, and be the last passenger on Frank Nestle's route.

That year revealed several of Regina's new unbeknown talents. She was aware of her ability to sketch well but, her grades in English and her comfort with spelling and grammar propelled her to write short stories for her classmate's pleasure. Marla, Jennette, Laura and Regina were very close friends who shared the same interests and grade point average. To her surprise they loved her writing so much until they seated themselves in the teacher's least possible line of view so their reading efforts during class would remain undetected. These girls found the stories intriguing, fascinating and the stories flowed with such ease. Her thoughts translated to paper with minimal effort and Regina wrote for hours just to provide her readers with new material each day. The intense expressions on their faces as they traveled through the many hand written pages and the lives of the characters she had created served as her much deserved reward.

Life was normal for her but, normal appeared strange because she was programmed early in life to expect chaos. The absence of such drama made regular rituals of every day life boring and unrewarding.

Subconsciously, she longed for the adrenaline surging through her body which was usually supplied by overwhelming excitement. However, life was as it was meant to be for her and required an adjustment of discomfort merely because she missed the edge that pain, suffering and injustice brought with it. These feelings tugged at her most inward core.

In early September of 1978, Regina, Carla and several of the neighbors sat in the backyard, faced Oakland Avenue and watched traffic into the complex and over across the street at the convenience store. Everyone but Regina and her neighbor-friend, Joan went inside and the two girls had become close enough to be considered family in each of their households. Two boys traveled in a baby blue, 1975 Lincoln Town Car and stopped on the side of Regina's apartment allowing just enough space for traffic to continue to flow.

"Hey, you ladies sure look nice." The young man, Charles, (on the passenger side) noticed the girls as soon as Ben made the left turn into Oakland Heights.

The young teen driver veered past his friend's head and concentrated on the young slender, medium complexioned girl with the long silky hair which flowed past her shoulder blades. Regina grew into quite a lovely young lady and as every year went by, she looked more like her mother. She had long lean but shapely legs which gained exposure from the adorable white shorts she wore and the white thong sandal on her extremely small feet for her 5'8" frame. Charles found interest in Joan because of her short neatly curled hair and light complexion. She was of medium build but, had extremely large, shapely calves and hips which made her much more appealing to him. Charles and Ben were juniors in high school that year. Joan remembered them because she had attended Williams Jr. High the previous year, directly across from Wilson High School where both boys attended. Ben and Charles exited the car and began to let their interests be known.

"Hi, boys. How are you?" Carla opened the door to inform the boys they were being watched.

"Hello, I'm Ben," he said as he reached for Carla's hand to shake it as a show of manners.

"Ben, Regina is my daughter. My name is Carla. How are you?"

"Fine. We were driving by and I noticed your beautiful daughter. I've stood here talking to her for a few minutes and she seems very smart too. You must be proud of her?" Ben was well groomed, very articulate and a gentleman.

The conversation peeked Carla's interest and she wanted to know more about the smooth talker. "Where do you live, Ben?" Carla asked.

"I live in Quimby which is on the top end of Irby Street," he quickly replied.

Carla was familiar with his area of town which was an upper middle class neighborhood. The more she conversed with the young man, the more she liked him.

"Who are your parents?"

"Ben and Clolita Dean. My father is Pastor of Trinity Baptist Church and my mother teaches 9th grade English at Wilson," Ben was proud to report.

"So, you attend Wilson High School?"

"Yes, Mam. I am a junior this year."

"I graduated from Wilson, valedictorian of my Class," she informed him.

Either he was truly interested or he was a superb actor and was worthy of nomination for an academy award. He won Carla over with his charm. Regina found his tall 6'3" slender physique just her style. Before then, Regina had not even thought about a boyfriend or dating even though she did have special feelings for the bus driver. Now, maturity had caused her sudden strong interests in Ben and it all came as quite a surprise to her as well as her mother.

"Ms. Carla, is that what you said your name was?" Ben wanted to address the adult properly.

"You can just call me Mrs. Wilson."

"Ms. Wilson, I really like your daughter. Would it be all right if I call her sometimes or maybe take her for a ride?" Ben had the charm gates wide open, now.

"You seem like a very nice young man but, Regina is only 15 years old. She is not old enough to date."

"I understand. Would you mind though if I just come and sit and talk with her or call her on the phone. I would just be happy if you would allow me to visit. We don't have to go anywhere and we can stay where you can see us." Ben was determined.

"You are a very persuasive young man, Ben. I can't see any harm in your calls or visits. It's been nice meeting you both." Carla returned inside.

Ben called every day and visited just as often. Charles and Joan dated briefly but, quickly lost interest in one another. Carla invited Ben in and he even shared meals with them while he developed a relationship with Carla. He had no reservations as he asked for permission to take Regina to his junior prom.

"Ben, I really like you a lot or I wouldn't have allowed you to keep company with my daughter even though she is not of proper dating age yet. I would not even consider this if it was anyone else but, I am trusting my daughter with you and you will have to answer to me if anything goes wrong. Do you understand what I'm telling you?" she asked the question as she glared at him over her brown framed glasses.

"Yes, Mam. What time should I have her back home?" He wanted to make sure that everything was understood because he did not want to betray the trust Carla had secured in him.

"Again, because you are the one asking, 1:00 a.m. is her curfew. What date is the prom?"

"April 30th. I will be wearing a gray tux if that will help you select a dress for her," Ben said thoughtfully.

CHAPTER 38

Prom arrival was much faster than either Regina or Ben imagined. Unbeknown to Regina, Ben enjoyed the time they spent conversing and holding hands but felt it was not enough for a committed relationship. That night meant more to Ben because he believed he would experience sex with the young woman whom he had done nothing more than kiss for the past eight months. But, Regina on the other hand was in love and naive. After all, this was her first relationship and all was perfect in her mind. She never expected any more than Ben had already offered and she automatically assumed he shared the same sentiment.

Carla purchased the fabric and pattern that Regina had chosen for her prom dress. She hired a seamstress and all the necessary preparations and alterations were completed. The dress was a pastel pink, form-fitted one piece which exposed Regina's back through an opening designed to show just between her shoulder blades and the side split extended from the hem of the dress to the right knee. There it hung, hours before the most important date of her life.

Regina spent all day preparing her long locks of sandy brown hair to frame her small delicate features perfectly and discovered yet another one of her many talents. She applied her make-up for the very first time just as it appeared on the cover model of the "Teen Magazine" which she had purchased for an example. Regina was beautiful. She had not over accentuated anything and she possessed a natural gift for duplicating the look and fashions of the experts. She was stunning and even Carla had to do a double take as she descended the last stair and entered the living room. The mother was pleased beyond her imagination and beamed with pride as Regina collected the evening bag lent to her from her mom's personal collection.

"Oh, Regina you look beautiful. I'll tell you the truth. When you bought the make-up, not ever having worn any, I was concerned. But you are a natural. You didn't hide or mask your features. You merely enhanced them. I have never seen you more beautiful," she admitted with tears welling in her eyes.

"Thanks, Mom, but you are my mother and you are supposed to say those things." Even Regina failed to realize the quality of work she had performed with her hair, make-up and nails.

"You know, I'm not one for giving compliments. So, I must truly be stunned," Carla explained.

Just as she spoke the last word from her mouth, the doorbell rang. It was 6:00 p.m. and Ben was obviously anxious because he was thirty minutes premature. Regina climbed the stairs once again to obtain the perfume her mother suggested she wear for the special occasion and upon her return, Ben sprang from the sofa where he occupied a seat and his eyes revealed his true impression of her. Those dark brown eyes were enlarged and full of excitement. His open mouth was evidence that he was in shear awe and really could not believe his eyes.

"Wow, you look beautiful! If I wasn't sure that you live here, I'd have to believe I had come to pick up the wrong date. Oh, God! You look so different, so grown up." Ben babbled on for another five minutes before he settled for just staring as she collected her purse and placed lipstick in it for potential touch ups.

"Thank you, Ben," she replied as she blushed. "You look very nice yourself, doesn't he, Mom?"

"Yes, I had already mentioned how handsome he looks," Carla admitted.

Regina never experienced anyone's vocalization of their opinion of her appearance, especially not her mother. It felt good. It was also the first time a young man had been so severely attentive and she decided at that very moment she desired for its continuance. Her inner beauty exuded as she walked with such assurance and perfect posture; anyone would easily have mistaken her for one that belonged on the cover of "Teen". Ben extended his arm and Regina graciously excepted the invitation for closeness as a Polaroid was snapped and Carla took one last glance at the couple before their date proceeded. The priceless expression on her face was of extreme pride and approval.

"Do you remember the curfew?" Carla directed the question to Ben.

"I will have her back home no later than 1:00, Mrs. Wilson."

"Have a good time tonight." Carla's advice was brief because she felt as though everything was totally under control. Ben opened the door of the Lincoln and closed it safely behind his prom queen. He wore the warmest smile as he swiftly moved around to the other side of the car to enter the vehicle.

"Are you ready?" Ben asked Regina as he took a hold of her hand.

"Yes, I'm ready," she replied.

Cinderella, without the wicked stepmother and sisters was the only suitable comparison for the enchantment of this young female. She had been transformed from a poor little girl into a beautiful princess and Ben was her prince. He came in the large expensive, Lincoln with leather seats to whisk her away, if only but for one night. The prom was her first and her friends were all of her age and therefore she had no expectations of what the experience should or would be.

Her only thought, "It will be magical because I am with Ben."

The festivities were held in the gymnasium. The theme was " A Starlit Night" and there were metallic silver stars hung from the rafters all over the gym, coupled with a 3/4 moon as well. They danced, mingled and Ben introduced Regina to all of his friends which produced instant envy from all the males there. The pride shown for her made Regina feel worth a million dollars as they danced again and again lost in each others eyes. Some friends whom were dateless stood and watched how harmoniously they moved to the love songs. Fortunately, Regina was an excellent dancer whatever the rhythm as she moved with such finesse and grace to the up tempo songs. Others were spellbound while the dance floor was captured by only the two of them.

It came the allotted time for photographs and Regina retreated to the rest room to ensure her make-up and hair had weathered the extreme dance experience. Because dancing required very little effort, there were minimal adjustments. Several young ladies who accompanied Regina in the rest room for the same purpose, complimented her dress and dance talent and it seemed as though the whole event had been designed especially for her; even though realistically she accepted that in fact was not the case. She returned to find Ben waiting by the door in attempts to foil any one's plot to steal Regina away. He managed to make her to feel so special, adored and alive. This was more than a prom for her, it was an awakening to life. Up until that very day, life had not offered very much.

Ben stood directly behind Regina and pulled her close to him. Secure was the feeling of being in his arms. Her 3" heels still failed to permit her height to remotely compete with his and the camera captured the enchanted expression of their eyes as evidence of what took place between the two of them. After several poses, Ben gently kissed Regina on the lips and led her to a secluded corner where he once again took her into his arms and stole her breath away. At that very moment, she experienced the feelings of a young woman, not a girl. Sensations she never felt raced within her. His body presented evidence of excitement as well and it startled Regina to the point where she was compelled to pull away slowly so as not to alert Ben. Her head swam, her heart raced and her breathing became erratic.

Carla never discussed the intimate details of a relationship between a man and a woman with Regina. She always appeared so much more wiser than her years, so Carla neglected pertinent information which was needed for Regina's development of a healthy relationship. Her mother's only advice on the matter was to abstain and the consequences of pregnancy were stressed firmly. Under no circumstances would Regina remain in her mother's household if she became impregnated. The very limited information she had gained was from high school, Sex Education classes which told her nothing about the emotional and physical affects which came along with a female being near a desired man. Carla had failed to even tell her about womanhood and its introduction presented itself during her menstrual cycle which had to be explained and attended by Ms. Dawn because its debut occurred during (tobacco season) the summer she worked with the Bacon's.

"What in the world is the matter with me?" She inquired of herself. "I should probably get some water or something to drink. I have danced for a long time and I need some liquids in my body. Yeah, that's it," she foolishly convinced herself.

Before her request for a beverage could be made, Ben pulled her close once more and this time the kiss was much more passionate. She could not stop him nor did she want to. He had never kissed her in that manner and the uncertainty of its origin lingered in the back of her mind.

"Ben has kissed me before, but never like this. Do I look that pretty? It must be the dress, hair and make-up," she told herself.

"Regina, are you hungry?" Ben interrupted her thoughts.

"Yes, a little."

"I have reservations at Red Lobster for 9:30. It's 9:00 and we will be right on time if we leave now," he urged.

Regina was relieved. Even though the kisses were exciting, the feelings that came along served to be unnerving and represented unfamiliar territory. She stationed herself across from Ben as they ate dinner and he was extremely quiet and possessed a strange glare in his eyes.

"Is everything all right? You've been so quiet on the ride here and you still haven't said much," she interrogated.

"Everything is perfect. I couldn't have asked for a better prom. I've always had to talk to you while your mother was around and I even had to sneak to get a kiss good-bye. It is so different tonight. We're grown and there are no limits and just looking at you makes me feel like I'm dreaming because the Regina I've been seeing never wore make-up or her hair down. You've always worn a ponytail. Now look at you! I just find it hard to believe that's all." Ben gave his best effort to explain but in actuality there were no words to express his true feelings.

After dinner, Ben went to Timrod Park off of Old Cemetery Road. Again, he tried to express to Regina what words could not. Finally, he gave in to the feelings and once again passionately kissed her. As his hands traveled to areas of her body she was not accustomed to, it was a foreign touch and she stopped him. The uneasiness soon progressed to extreme discomfort. The reality of the situation was, he was in lust and she was in love.

CHAPTER 39

Regina looked up at the ceiling as she thought of how long it had been since she had heard Ben's voice. Prom night was already a month in history and she refused to believe Ben had left the relationship without the reason for its demise discussed. After she insisted not to explore the avenue of sex on that night, she longed for his innocent kiss good-bye. More realistically, she craved the prom night kisses and when she managed enough courage to phone him, she was unable to reach him. And he chose not to return her many messages. She was so naive. She actually had no inkling why the relationship abruptly came to such a screeching halt. All her heart was able to reveal was that she loved him and the pain she believed would never diminish.

"Regina, you've been in bed all day. It's a beautiful day out and it's not like you to lay around," Carla mentioned.

Regina had no desire to talk to her mother about the pain she was feeling because talking had never solved anything with them before. She dared not believe her mother actually cared what ailed her beyond the fact that one of the twin beds which she still occupied remained unmade. Carla never made a habit to question her daughter if things appeared strange or out of the ordinary but, she could only exemplify what was shown to her which means the distant behavior had passed down through generations.

Her love for Ben superseded any experience she ever had and that revelation came as a surprise to the young teen-ager as she remembered some of the hell of her early childhood. Nothing compared to the excruciating, uncontrollable, deep rooted pain which plagued her heart.

"This love thing is not what it's cracked up to be. I'll never fall in love again with anyone!" She struggled to recant her statement. "But, everything is supposed to get better with time," she mumbled. "I still love him! I still hurt," were the repeated thoughts which casually crossed her mind when she allowed it to drift for a much needed break from her homework.

She refused to confide in her friends outside or at school time and Carla was old fashioned in her belief that the telephone was for adult use only. Ben was the

131

one she shared her rationed phone time with because he asked her mother's permission directly. Therefore, Regina never felt the need to distribute or exchange telephone numbers with others and when she did, the conversations were rare and brief.

One night, crying in her bed, she decided at the end of ninth grade at Southside; she would transfer to Wilson where Ben would be a senior and she a sophomore. She had to be near him and she hoped his seeing her on a daily basis, might generate a chance to begin their relationship anew. But, that proved to be more of a heartache and not a solution. The summer lingered and was much less eventful which may have been attributed to the love struck teen's anxiety and eagerness for the school term break to be over. There was nothing worth experiencing that remotely measured up to the importance of rekindling her romance with Ben. Even the usual walks with Joan decreased because she found solace in wallowing in her thoughts of the man she loved. The new school year finally arrived and the new found hope of regaining her lost love dimmed at a very quick pace.

"I'm not with him and I feel like my heart is going to explode every time I pass him in the hall or see him on campus!" Regina had just looked into his face from a distance down a long hallway as he smiled and conversed with a shapely young female classmate. It was more than she could endure. She opened a book and pretended to be in search of something as not to be noticed by him while walking in route to her French class. This continued for months.

As years before, school served as an escape from her problems. She focused on schoolwork and homework rather than thoughts about the embedded pain which haunted her daily. The comforting plans of the long dreaded summer had become a nightmare and though her grades remained above average, her heart became more burdened and heavy. She possessed absolutely no power to bring him back because she was unaware of what really caused the rift in the relationship and brought it to its knees. She actually believed that her inexpensive everyday wardrobe was the culprit and the one night as Cinderella fueled his disinterest.

Regina battled against her need for a diversion and recognized that just school work would not fully provide relief. So, she focused on flag team try-outs and found it most enjoyable. There were new people to meet and associations to make. There were practices, games, parades and competitions and very little time to concentrate on anything else. The band participation was just what the doctor ordered for the broken hearted and everything about the flag team made her feel alive, vibrant and confident! For the first time in quite some time, her heart was not heavy. Actually, it was light, giddy and free to explore yet another talent Regina found where she was not required to put forth a large effort to accomplish. And yet there were rave reviews and great benefits. She was seeing life through a new prospective and tackling it with zeal. She also conquered a Junior Varsity Cheerleader position as captain the same year. She survived football miraculously due to both activities' utilization of half-time and when that season ceased, basketball served as a much needed break. By no means was she suddenly cured of the sickness called "Loving Ben," but the severity of the pain was lessened and the wonderful lessons about herself surfaced from the inward search for happiness. The young woman also found consolation in the fact that she was not the only one left in love with Ben. There were others.... many, many, many others.

One of the revelations regarding the secrets to life was exposed to her. "The world doesn't revolve around me. Life is what you make of it and it can be good if you make the best of every opportunity for happiness," she smiled to herself as if someone had actually spoken the words audibly and she intently listened.

"Yes, life has taken a turn and you are forced to chose and turn with it to see what other options might be available." But, the newly traveled road she found also exposed some evidences she was familiar with but desired to suppress.

She transformed into the kind of flag-girl and cheerleader whom would become the pride and joy of any mother. She practiced extremely hard, not just to be good but to be recognized for her expertise which was her motivation to bring practice flags home. She was dedicated and focused. And yet, unlike other parents, Carla chose not to be a part of the exciting time in her daughter's life. She refused to attend any games or competitions and she witnessed her daughter's excellence during one parade which was the only encounter her mother desired to have with the band or athletics. There was no family other than Carla in Florence and therefore, there was no support, outward show of interest or love for her to others. The pain remained hidden and Regina just assumed her mother's age hindered her from taking an interest as other younger parents displayed to their children. The age difference between her parent and those of her piers was an embarrassment and a curse she often thought. She wondered why things had to be the way they were? But, the self-pride she discovered overshadowed her desire for her mother's attention during this era and she managed to be graced with a new found freedom, her independence.

CHAPTER 40

"Hey, girl!" Joan shouted to gain Regina's attention as she approached the practice field through the band room. "Where have you been? You are usually at flag practice long before I get here and they are about to pick this year's squad."

"Am I late?" Regina sarcastically inquired.

"No, but you're always the first one here. Anyway, I'm glad you're here now 'cause there......" Her thought was interrupted by the previous year flag captain as she blew her whistle in hopes of silence. The names of the twelve 1979-80 squad were announced and both joy and pain pierced Regina's heart. She would be allowed once again to enjoy the camaraderie of the band/flag team but, Joan had been overlooked. They shared every game, practice and special function together and the source of their current close bond was in jeopardy of becoming a dividing factor.

She walked over to Joan to console her but all time permitted for was, "I'm sorry. I'll call you later."

The new team bestowed the honor of not only being on the flag team again, she was named co-captain with another close classmate. To her surprise, Joan continued her attendance of band practice and observed in order to maintain walks home with Regina. Bitterness never developed and Joan was mature enough not to allow her inactivity with the flag team to drive a wedge between them. Extremely relieved, Regina accepted her friend as the support system she had been deprived of for years and after practice one afternoon, Joan gave mention of a surprise.

"What kind of a surprise?" Regina asked in anticipation.

"There is somebody who is dying to meet you."

"Who?" Regina frowned. Her imagination would not fathom anyone thinking that much of her. She was aware that she was well-liked but, Joan made it sound as though she was of major celebrity status.

"He's headed this way now," as she pointed in the direction of a brand new, dark metallic-blue, 1980 Pontiac Firebird. The car took her breath away as well as the owner's request to meet her.

"What does he want to meet me for?"

"Girl, you're crazy. What do you mean, what does he want to meet you for? He's interested in you. He was in the band last year and since he's graduated he's been watching the band and you. Here he comes."

"Hey, Joan," the young man approached the two females.

"Hey, Reggie. This is my friend, Regina."

"Hi, Regina. He spoke calmly but his eyes viewed her as though she was a peppermint destined for a dry, scratchy throat.

Joan and Reggie held the conversation and Regina awkwardly stood silent. They conversed about friends they had in common and the gossip which was associated with knowing them.

"Look guys, I've got to get home. I've got homework so, I'll see you later Joan," Regina stated as she was already in process of turning away.

"Where are you going? I'm coming!" she addressed Regina. "Reggie, I'll talk to you tomorrow," Joan then said as she issued a strange look to him.

"I haven't' had a chance to get to know Regina yet. Can I give you girls a ride home?" he asked with a smirk. "That way you can get to your homework a little faster."

Before Regina had opportunity to reply, Joan accepted the invitation and was headed in the direction of the car. She reluctantly followed and Joan strategically placed herself in the back seat so as to force Regina into the front next to Reggie. He was very slender and not as tall as she had a passion for; and was dark complexioned and not her idea of handsome either. But, she never knew anyone with such a magnificent piece of machinery and because there was more of an interest in it than Reggie, she allowed him to chauffeur her. She preferred the attention he gave her, too. When the three had entered the vehicle, groups of students standing around after practice pointed and talked. Reggie was popular last year and was taking time off since graduation to decide his path in life. The car was a graduation present from his parents and it was quite the attention-getter.

"Hey, man, thanks for the ride home. I'll catch you later," Joan yelled and she rushed into her apartment leaving Regina unattended with Reggie.

She managed to get out of the car and turned only to thank him for the ride but was interrupted. "Regina, can we stand outside and talk for a minute? I know you have homework but, just for a little while."

Carla noticed from her bedroom window that Regina was escorted by a young man. She was actually gladdened by the sight too because even though she had never discussed things with her daughter, she believed Ben's mysterious disappearance devastated her. The seasoned pro rationalized what happened or better yet what had not happened. She was pleased that her girl refrained yet, she was not totally cold hearted and related to her daughter's first time love experience. Since Ben, Regina not so much as mentioned boys or even desired to date. But, to see her with Reggie was a relief. It was a sign of healing or so it seemed anyway.

As they stood in front of the apartment door, " Regina, you are very good with the flag team. I watched you last year and believe it or not you've managed to get even better. You have a natural talent for it I guess."

"Thanks. I really like it." She gave a short but sweet reply. Although normally talkative, she found herself intimidated and shy; not quite sure of herself.

"You're so quiet. Normally, you're so bubbly. What's wrong?" He seemed genuinely concerned.

"I don't know. I guess I'm wondering what you want from me. Why did you want to meet me so bad?"

"I think you're so pretty. I like everything about you, your hair, height, your voice and the way you giggle. You seem to be a very nice person and I just want to get to know you. I know it sounds crazy but, I love your smile and the way you walk. Just seeing you brightens up my day," Reggie answered.

Regina could appreciate Reggie's impression of her. Ironically, he had just described her feelings for Ben but, naïveté gave way to reality and Ben was merely her first love and there was bound to be others. Reggie maybe not, but because he seemed to care for her, she found him worth while.

CHAPTER 41

Reggie took advantage of every opportunity given him to spend time with Regina. He could be depended on like clockwork to pick her up after practice and he talked with Carla during the completion of her homework assignments. What dedication! Both Regina and Reggie loved the attention even though they had different motives. They served a very important purpose to one another, he was graced with the girl of his dreams and she gained the positive male attention she was starved of since her relationship with Ben. Reggie was granted an open invitation for Sunday dinner and he in turn invited her to share time with his parents at his father's church and their home. His father was a sweetheart and a godly minister. His mother, on the other hand, was very judgmental.

"Who are your parents?" Mrs. Sawyer asked inquisitively.

"Joseph Ulzler and Carla Wilson. She eagerly supplied the answer hoping to gain Mrs. Sawyer's approval.

His mother's smile gave way for a brief moment to a look of concern before the smile returned but somehow not as sincere. Her sudden discomfort, fidgeting with the magazine in her lap and the frequent weight shift from side to side before continuing her line of questioning gave every indication that she had lost interest.

"Where do you live, Regina?"

"I live in Oakland Heights Apartments on Oakland....." She was interrupted before her reply was finished.

"I know where they are," Mrs. Sawyer snapped as if to let Regina know the conversation needed not continue.

Regina remembered the same behavior from Ben's mother when they first met but, realization that her neighborhood was considered low class escaped her. She knew her home to be an elevation in comparison to what she was previously accustomed to. But both Ben and Reggie's parents were viewed as upper middle class. And in the mind of this northern school girl, they were rich yet, in their minds she was not.

Reggie was an only child. He was spoiled past rotten and there was no other way but his. The Sawyers provided much encouragement for his thought process and because of his possession of fine cars and money, he purchased his way in every aspect of life. His parent's home was located across the street from the school and to secure his relationship with Regina, he stationed the car on school property before practice ended and left the spare keys with her which ensured her return to him. Meanwhile, Regina basked in the fact that no one had ever trusted her with as much and she loved being equipped with a new sports car. That show of trust boosted her self confidence, self-worth and not to mention, her popularity increase.

It was Friday evening and Reggie picked up Regina from school early because there was no band practice. They went in pursuit of fast food and stopped at his parent's who had gone to a church function which meant they would be home alone. The petting became passionate and Regina became scared. She vividly remembered how excited Ben became the night of prom and then he dismissed her as nothing more than a notion. Even though Reggie's reaction to her was the same as Ben, Regina was physically unattracted and not aroused. She was pleased with her lack of sexual interest however, because her fondness of Reggie had not remotely escalated to those feelings for her first love.

"What's the matter?" Reggie was surprised when the kiss ended so bluntly.

"I can't do this. I want you to take me home right now, Reggie!"

"What did I do? I'm sorry for whatever I did. Did I do something wrong?" Reggie was confused.

"It's not you. I'm just not comfortable here in your parents house while they are away," she scrambled for an excuse.

"Oh, is that all. Come on, they won't be back for hours. You don't have a thing to worry about except making me happy," he replied as he reached to draw her nearer to him once more.

"I'm not staying here. Please Reggie, let's just go back to my house."

They got into the car and Reggie turned to her suddenly. "Regina you don't like me do you?"

"Come on. I like you a lot but, you seem like you want to get real serious with me and I'm not ready for that. I care about you Reggie and I really appreciate how nice you are to me but, I'm just not ready for it to go any farther. I mean, I'm not ready to have sex." There, it was out in the open.

"Are you not ready to do it or are you just not ready to do it with me? We've been seeing each other for four months now. It's time. I let you drive my car, I'd give you anything you want and have done so. Why won't you give me the one thing I want?"

"So, that's why you've been so nice to me. Is that why you have spent every day of the last four months with me? All you wanted to do was get close enough to me to get sex from me. Is that what you are telling me, Reggie?"

"No, no, no! Regina, I am a man. I like you and I want you. That's what men and women do." He stared at her as if he could not believe his need to explain his feelings to her.

But, she was as determined not to experience sex as he was to have her. The affects of Ben's kisses were not there and she knew the missing ingredient was love, at least on her part.

"Reggie, I'm scared O.K. I've never had sex before and I really don't want to. Do you just like me because you want my body or do we have something more?"

"You know we have something more! Why would you even ask me that? I don't like you! I love you," he blurted the words out to his own surprise.

No one had ever told her they loved her. Not in her entire sixteen years of living had her father, mother, siblings or friends openly expressed any kind of feelings of emotion for her. She began to cry.

"I didn't mean to make you cry! What's the matter?"

"No, you didn't. I've just never been told that by anyone before." And for the second time in her life, circumstances forced her reflection on her early childhood years. The more she shared, the more she cried. Reggie listened intently and was overwhelmed with emotion. They were drawn closer that night but, not in the way he had hoped. However, he managed to get closer to her. Now, he was not just her boyfriend but a confidant and now occupied a place in her heart. He just had not yet hit the bulls-eye. They continued their talk until 12:00 a.m. and he kissed her gently on the lips and wiped away the remnant of tears that flowed from her eyes. They parted and Reggie found himself intrigued by her all the more.

CHAPTER 42

C hristmas' quick arrival placed extreme pressure of an appropriate gift for Reggie. Their dating had just begun at the first of the school year and she feared him mistaking the value of her gift to him as somehow being equivalent to that of their relationship. On the other hand, she definitely desired not to cheapen their friendship either. After much debate and conversations with Joan, she was definite with her choice of a brand-name wool sweater which she beautifully gift wrapped herself. Reggie, on the other hand, went to an extraordinary extreme. A 1/3 karat diamond solitaire was purchased in hopes that with a promise of marriage he would find her more willing to cooperate with his sexual plans for her.

Christmas day proved to be less than a joyous occasion. Once his gift to her was opened, there entered a twenty-ton weight placed on her shoulders along with a ring for her finger. Marriage....she had never thought of it and was angry because she was forced to do so as a junior in high school. She viewed, through her mother's experiences, the institution as nothing more than a hardship and headache and was determined to avoid the same for herself. But, she did not want to torment Reggie and had to find a way to show him this was not the route to take.

"So, what you think?" Reggie was eager for a response.

"It's beautiful," she replied in a low and distant voice.

He kissed her on the cheek in anticipation of her showering him with affection. It never happened. She just gazed blankly down at the ring in the box and said nothing.

"I know it's beautiful but, let's see what it looks like on your finger," Reggie stated as he removed the ring from its perch and slowly pushed it onto her left hand.

Suddenly, there came a deep ache in her heart. She had no desire for him and she did not want the ring. And because she had allowed her silence to be the interpretation for acceptance, she now had a greater task than if she had immediately refused. As time went by, the ache continued to fester until there was no

140

room for politeness.

"I don't want this! I don't want to marry you and I don't want to hurt you! Our talks have been nice but that's all it's been. Why do you insist on making more of this relationship than there is? Why did you have to make things this way? Why did you have to push your feelings on me? Why, Reggie?"

He was startled because he was caught up in the thought of their marriage until he failed to see there was not equal joy from Regina. She was not happy. She was now angry.

"You don't want to marry me?" he managed to get the words past the large lump in his throat which strangled him.

"Look, I am only 16 years old....."

"You'll be 17 in a few months."

"I know how old I will be in a few months!" She snapped. "You just have to mess up everything. I don't want to get married! Can you get that through your head or are you too busy being happy for yourself that it doesn't matter what I say?" She slipped the ring off her finger and handed it to him.

"I can't take it! I bought it for you and there is nothing I want it for other than for you to wear it. It's your mother isn't it? She's the one who talked you out of it? You really want this but it's her! I know she has just been cordial to me but she really doesn't like me. I haven't said anything before now because I knew you were strong minded or at least I thought you had a mind of your own. You can't let your mama run your life for the rest of your life. All you have to do is make it until you get to be 18. That's not very far away and we can be together."

"Reggie, stop blaming my mother. It's not her. She told you in front of me that she thought it wasn't the right time but if that's what we wanted she wouldn't stand in our way. It's easier to blame her than to accept that I don't want this. What have I said to anyone about being engaged to you? Nothing. Don't you find that odd for someone who is supposed to be so happy. Have I smiled? What have I done that would make you think this is what I want?"

"You took the ring!" He shouted loud enough for Carla to become alarmed and escaped the comfort of her bedroom to insure that her presence was known.

"Reggie, what are you so upset about?" Carla was inquisitive.

"You talked her out of it didn't you? You never wanted me with her anyway and as sure as I stand here, I know you've been working on her to change her mind."

"Who in hell do you think you are talking to! I know you are upset but you might want to take a minute to collect yourself because if you keep talking to me in that tone, son, you will be getting up off the floor." Carla glared at him to confirm receipt of her threatening message.

"He's mad because I gave him back the ring and told him I wasn't ready to be anyone's wife," Regina interrupted to give both Reggie and Carla a window of opportunity to cool down.

She knew Reggie had never witnessed the Carla who enjoyed and invited

141

physical confrontations and it had been a long time since her taking pleasure in one. She also noticed how her mother kept her right hand in her pocket of her robe, remained standing the entire time which made it obvious she meant business and was carrying her gun.

"Reggie, look I want you to go," Regina was speaking quickly. "We can talk about this later. I don't mean to hurt you, but you have got to go, now!" She kept watch of her mother's right hand and glanced back and forth between the two of them. She found it necessary to affix her eyes to keep watch on the hand that she knew was anxious and ready to defend the house.

"I'm going to ask you nicely. Regina has asked you and now I'm telling you that you have over-stayed your welcome. You have disrespected me in my house and it would be to your benefit to leave now while you have the chance to do so under your own power. This is the last warning!" Carla exclaimed as she took two steps toward him.

By this time, tears streamed down Regina's face and Reggie noticed Carla's right hand and the imprint of the gun. His movements became much more hurried as he collected his coat to leave. As he walked out the door he yelled to Regina.

"I won't give up that easy. I'll never give up! You will be mine, do you hear me?"

Carla slammed the door behind him. "I don't ever want that boy back in this house again do you understand me?" She spoke with such intensity until all Regina managed was a nod in agreement before the misinterpretation of uneasiness was mistook for anger.

"Girl, I taught you to answer me not to nod your head! You're not deaf nor mute!"

"I don't want him here ever again either." Regina meant it but she also knew it was the only statement that would have calmed her mother.

CHAPTER 43

Regina replayed the meeting between herself and Reggie through her mind like that of a well promoted movie trailer for the rest of the entire weekend. "I wish I'd handled things better," she thought. "But, he kept pressuring and pushing and well.....it's all said and done now. I've got to get out of here or I'll be late for school. God, please don't let him come after school to talk to me. Let him be so mad about Friday night until he never wants to speak to me again."

She walked up to her locker to get books for her first period class and there Reggie stood waiting. Her heart raced and it was quickly decided that it would be better to go to class without her book than to deal with him. And she was far enough in the distance to get to her next period down a side hall. She evaded him, but only for the moment. After English, at the outside exit to the next class, she stumbled right into him.

"Hey, I was hoping we could talk before your next class? Look, I'm not mad at you, none of this is your fault. Anybody would do what their mother wanted right now. We will just stay calm and see each other when we can until you can sign the papers for yourself."

"I'm trying to get to class, Reggie. I have a test. I don't want to talk to you about this right now. Please just leave me alone?"

"I'll never leave you alone. I love you. But, just let me walk you to class."

They walked to the other side of the campus in silence. Half-way across the yard, a teacher yelled to him.

"Reggie, what are you doing on school property?"

Regina was overcome with relief because the PE Coach saved her even if only for a little while. Driver's Education did not last in its entirety and after the completion of the practice written test, everyone reported to the football field where the school vehicle was placed for basic maneuvers. The class was dismissed from the field and she was confident he was gone by now.

Reggie saw a friend who was a guidance work-study student and asked for Regina's schedule. She easily obliged him with no questions asked. His strategy was to meet her after third period because lunch would not allow him enough time to talk. But, patience was not a virtue for him and the door of Regina's third period class door was often left open as relief of the extreme year-round heat in the room. She listened intently as the teacher lectured but her attention was soon broken by Reggie standing outside of the teacher's range of view but directly in hers as she sat on the first row in front of the door. Her heart sank and she tried not to let him know he had been identified but several of her classmates, aware of their dating, assisted in making sure she acknowledged his presence.

The stalking continued for a solid week. Each class, she feared there would be an encounter with Reggie. "I've got to approach this better. I can't be nasty to him because he's just not getting it. I'll try to be nice and calm about things and they'll get better then. I dare not tell my mother, she's upset still about the other Friday night and I really can't talk to anyone else because I don't want to embarrass him in front of our friends. It will be over soon. Just be patient," she told herself.

Her calm, nice attitude only added fuel to an already blazing inferno. He convinced himself that she was breaking instead of hearing that she just wanted to return to friendship. All he gathered was that she was not angry so things were back on track. He brought her lunch from her favorite places just to buy time (lunch period) with Regina.

"Reggie, I don't want Wendy's. I paid for my lunch last week and didn't eat not once. You don't have to buy me lunch every day. I want to eat with my friends because I haven't spent any time with them in a while."

"Well, just eat this since I've already bought it. I know you don't want me to waste my money. Don't you enjoy spending your lunch with me?"

She ate the lunch quietly while she listened to his plans for the future. She was unaware of whether she felt sick from the food or from his dreamland conversation.........it was definitely the conversation.

After two weeks of sharing Wilson High campus with a previous year graduate, she became increasingly annoyed. He brought donuts, candy, cookies, supposedly to shower her with affection. But, strange things began to take place and she had no idea what was happening. She gradually had no control of her thoughts or feelings. While she was away from him, she despised him. But she no longer could avoid him. Her heart hated to see his face but somehow, she ended up allowing him to become a part of her school activities. She introduced him to the Driver's Education instructor and he was allowed access to the driving field where the students practiced. She really felt confused because she had no desire for his company and she actually resented his being there.

"Reggie, I've tried to be nice. I thought we could be friends but we can't. You keep talking like we are getting married and it is really getting on my nerves. You are following me around my school and you are a distraction because you won't let me have a minute of peace. You don't seem to understand I do not love you, I have never told you I love you and yet you seem to think your loving me is enough. Frankly, your love scares me. It frightens me now since you have made it your lifelong ambition to spend every waking moment with me. I don't have time for this. I need to get my education and go on with my life which, by the way, does not include you. I've asked you every way I know how to leave me alone. I can't even go to lunch by myself. You are so possessive and I feel like there is something very wrong with you. I've told you in a nasty way. I've blurted it out. I've even taken the nice approach and you don't hear me. I want you to hear me today, Reggie! I want you to leave me alone! I don't want your lunches and I don't want your ring. I don't want anything from you. I don't mean to yell at you but you just don't hear me otherwise. I've tried to do things quietly so you wouldn't be embarrassed and you've taken it as some sick clue that we're a couple. For the last time, I'm begging you to just leave me alone!"

The entire class heard the long speech Regina preached to Reggie and he walked away with tears in his eyes. She was saddened by her obligation to go to such extremes although she felt a false sense of relief as his shoulders slumped and he slowly drifted away.

Carla was filled in on the events of the last three weeks. Regina told her of Reggie's insistence upon intruding on her school life but, she was merely having an informative chat with her mother of how she handled her own situation. Carla however, was not going to miss an opportunity to take a jab at Reggie. She grossly overreacted and went to the school principal who was also a fellow church member. She demanded the school take a more aggressive part and responsibility in keeping Reggie away from Regina. Even though the traps were set for him, Reggie worked through mutual friends who thought the couple was just going through rough times. Regina became afraid to go to basketball games or dances. Carla noticed how isolated she suddenly became. She accepted no phone calls and stopped participating in extracurricular activities except cheering and the joy in that had dissipated.

Four to five weeks passed and then unexplained things became a regular occurrence. Regina suffered sharp, shooting, piercing pains which raced through her brain while in class and at home. Sounds of people talking seemed muffled, slurred and distorted. She became dizzy and without very much warning, blackouts accompanied by some sort of seizure-like behavior took place. The episodes grew more frequent with each passing day and teachers and students alike were genuinely concerned about her health.

One Thursday, while in Social Studies, Regina listened for the instructions of an upcoming project and then, sharp pains pierced her head like an assassin's bullet. The pains' initial description of headaches was not accurate yet, the only one that came close at the time. They moved swiftly seemingly from one side of the brain to the other, never one single pain but several moving with lightening speed simultaneously within one to two second intervals. After the blackout, she fell to the floor from her desk and Ms. Alston instructed two male classmates to carry her to the nurse's office in their arms.

Carla took Regina to their family doctor who believed in medicating and seldom searched for a cause. He prescribed medications which kept her heavily sedated. She slept day and night and Carla's fear for her daughter compelled her to do two things. She found another physician who ran a battery of different tests. Nothing was found. She paid another visit to the principal and he arranged to have all Regina's lessons from every class and tests sent home to deter grade declination. Carla also witnessed several of the blackouts herself and was terrified by their frequency and severity.

Meanwhile, as small as she was, Regina lost weight. She went from 5'8", 114 lbs. to 102 lbs. within a month's time. Her skin darkened two shades and her appearance was as of someone who was terminally ill. Carla feared for her daughter's life and the caring and nurturing Regina desired since early childhood, ironically came at this time. There were more referrals to specialists and more episodes. She refused church attendance or even visits to the corner store because of her condition which automatically bound Carla to home as well.

Regina had difficulty sleeping nights once Carla removed her from the sedatives. She progressively became worse. She screamed when she saw spots moving all over the bed even though her sheets were actually solid in color and woke at night to hallucinations of bugs entirely covering and crawling along the walls, windows, floors and bed. The successful calming of Regina came through scriptures read to her until she fell asleep for a maximum of an hour only to awake to the same repetitive cycle.

One Sunday morning, Carla convinced Regina to try to go to church to receive special prayer regarding her condition. The teen-ager was reluctant yet wanted desperately to regain her health. Carla's friend, whom Regina affectionately called "Aunt Nancy", made a comment to Carla which both shocked and stunned her into an answered prayer.

"Carla, that child is very sick. Just looking at her skin and her eyes, there is something very wrong with her. You'd better get her some help and I mean right away!"

"I've taken her to all kinds of doctors and they can't find anything. I've run from this hospital to the other and every kind of test under the sun has been done on her. They can't find anything!" Carla was frustrated and scared.

"You don't find that strange? I do. The child's complexion has changed, she's obviously lost weight as if she wasn't small enough to begin with, she has dark circles around her eyes which are glassy enough to be used as mirrors. How can the doctors be satisfied that just because they haven't found anything, that nothing serious is wrong with her? Carla I'm begging you. If you don't get her some help, this girl is going to die."

"I've done everything I know how. What do you have in mind?" Carla stared at her dear friend as though her life depended on the answer rather than her daughter's.

"There is this lady that I've heard people talk about. They say she's good. Her name is Lady Sarah and I'm sure she can help you. I'll call you later with the telephone number and you can take her over to see her right away."

"Who is Lady Sarah?" Carla was not familiar with the woman.

"She's a spiritual advisor and healer. When you can't find a cure physically, Lady Sarah is known for healing. As soon as I get home and get the number, I will call you and you need to see her today if she can give you an appointment. Make sure you tell her how ill Regina is and she will make time for you."

"So, you're telling me that this woman deals with witchcraft? You know that I don't believe in that mess! She doesn't deal in witchcraft does she?"

"She doesn't practice it but she can cancel whatever the spell that has been placed on a person. Now, I know this might sound crazy to you Carla, but you said yourself you've tried everything and nothing else has worked. What do you have to lose? Anyone with eyes can see something is terribly wrong with that child. For her sake, just give it a try."

Nancy was a woman of her word and as soon as she got home and retrieved the number she had tucked away in a secret place, she called Carla and gave it to her. "Be sure to tell her I told you to call. She doesn't just deal with anybody and she's not in it for the money."

Nancy's statement informed Carla that her dear friend had not just merely heard of this woman. Carla dialed the number up to four digits and then hung up the phone.

"This is crazy! I can't believe Nancy believes in this. I really need to be more careful who I become friends with. You could never have convinced me in a million years that she believed in witchcraft. She sure had me........" She continued to look at the name and number Nancy had given; written on the inside of the yellow pages cover. "But, what if that's what is really wrong with Regina. What if this stuff is real? What if Reggie decided she wasn't going to live to love anybody? That black bastard would do something evil like that too. I knew there was a reason why I didn't like him! Carla, stop talking to yourself. Either you are going to call or you are going to continue to wonder what is going on. If this doesn't work, then I can at least say that I ruled out everything."

She dialed the number again and listened for the three rings which were followed by a woman's soft, hypnotic voice. "Hello?"

"Hello. Is this Lady Sarah?" Carla still was hesitant but knew she had traveled too far past the point of no return to stop now.

"Yes it is. Who's calling?"

"I am a friend of Nancy Bennett and my daughter, Regina, is very ill. I've taken her to every doctor, specialist and hospital in town and no one can find out what's wrong with her. They all agree she is ill but have no idea what the problem is. She looks so bad and she's loosing weight even though she's very small to begin with. Nancy said if I didn't bring her to see you right away she believes Regina will die. Can you please see us today?" The urgency in Carla's tone increased with every spoken word.

"Yes, I can see you now. Here is my address and don't wait, come right now!" Lady Sarah spoke with the same urgency which somehow brought comfort. She wrote down the address hurriedly, dressed comfortably and drove with haste to the spiritual advisor's house/office. It was a small dwelling with all types of spiritual trinkets such as crosses and praying hands everywhere. The furniture was expensive and the arrangement of her spiritual things possessed an eclectic feel. Carla and Regina both were visibly nervous.

"Come on in and have a seat over by the lamp," Lady Sarah directed. "Now, you must be Regina? You are not sick, Regina. Someone is making you sick. You are not going to die and you will be well within the next week if you and your mother do what I tell you to do. You must do everything that I tell you and you can't leave anything out. You can not ask me any questions but you must believe everything that I tell you. If you ask me questions, I will not answer. But, you can believe that everything I tell you will answer every possible question you might have about your condition or the circumstances around it. Do you understand?"

Carla looked over toward Regina and then her attention went back to Lady Sarah. "I understand."

Lady Sarah looked at Regina and began to speak. "There is a man who is older than you and he loves you. He loves you more than his own life. It is an unnatural love because he would go to any measures to have you. He wanted to kill himself before he met you but you became his reason to live. You are not with him presently and he insisted on giving you food. He adorned you with lavish gifts and trusted you so freely. The things were a trap to keep you interested. He knows you don't love him but he loves you enough for the both of you. You have stopped all contact with him which is good but, his efforts to get to you will not stop. I have some oil that I am going to pray over and then touch you where I feel you have been affected and you will be freed from the clutches of evil as long as you don't call his name during the healing period. The name will open up your mind to what he tried to achieve."

Then she removed her short heavy-set body from the chair she had occupied since the beginning of the visit and reached into a drawer of the end table for a small bottle of oil. She placed the oil on her fingertip and marked a cross on Regina's forehead. "Your head will hurt no more, in the name of Jesus!" She yelled. "The evil visions will stop! You will go back to school and you will live!........ Ms. Wilson, you must guard her from evil and leave no gate open for its return. Here is something to place under her pillow." She handed Carla a brown, palm-sized, drawstring bag with something inside and the small bottle of blessed oil.

"Put this on her forehead before she goes to bed at night and when she wakes up in the morning for the next seven days. Repeat what I have just said as you put the oil on her head day and night. Continue the scriptures I have given you and she will be good as new this time next week. You must go now. There is no charge, just go!"

148